FAR and AWAY
True Brit:
Beatrice, 1940

ISBN: 978-1-932926-18-7

Artemesia Publishing, LLC
9 Mockingbird Hill Rd
Tijeras, New Mexico 87059
info@artemesiapublishing.com
www.apbooks.net

FAR and AWAY
True Brit:
Beatrice, 1940

by

Rosemary Zibart

Illustrated by:

George Lawrence

Kinkajou Press
Albuquerque, New Mexico
www.apbooks.net

To Jake
who makes everything possible.

To Sergei and Brandon
who bring me such delight.

In memory of ...

Tanya
who gave me a sense of the journey.

And Jaenet
whose enthusiasm for this story was key.

Chapter One

Only Great-Aunt Augusta spoke up against the plan. As usual, we had gathered for tea at her big elegant house in Mayfair on Wednesday at 4 p.m. sharp. White-haired and stout, Great-Aunt Augusta had made it quite clear she wouldn't allow the War to interfere with her teatime. Of course we each carried a gas mask to her home, just in case. The gas masks were made of smelly rubber and I dreaded using one but we feared a poison gas attack might come at any time.

Hearing the news of my trip, Great-Aunt Augusta looked appalled. "You don't mean to say you're going to send Beatrice to the United States!" she said. "The girl will surely lose all her manners. She'll return chewing gum and wearing lipstick."

"There are some things rather worse than chewing gum," Father replied, smiling at me kindly. "We want Beatrice to be absolutely safe."

I knew what Father was speaking about. Beginning on 7 September, we saw the air over London fill with Nazi planes. Horrid screaming bombs began falling from the sky, forcing thousands of us to crowd underneath the streets in the Underground. Since then, we huddled together every night in the dark listening to the explosions. Each morning we climbed out, fearful that a beloved house or church or shop had been demolished.

In some neighborhoods, block after block of buildings had been destroyed. Where there had once been a row of lovely homes, nothing remained but rubble, broken glass and dishes, smashed furniture, even soggy bed mattresses and torn clothes. People seldom bothered to go back to bombed houses for their belongings. It was too dangerous and too sad.

The vicious Nazis imagined they could destroy our wonderful little country of England, but they should have known better. Every Brit who was old enough was either bravely fighting or steadfastly protecting the country. Like my 17-year-old brother, Willy, who was in the Home Guard. Every night, he helped guide ambulance drivers through the wrecked city. Though only twelve, I wished I could go along and help also.

Yet now Mother was insisting I leave the city. The sooner, the better.

"I won't go. I won't go," I hissed through clenched teeth. "You can't make me."

But Mother was firm. "Darling, thousands of children have

left already for places in the country or abroad. You simply can't stay here another minute."

She rang up the Children's Overseas Reception Board, which was placing children in homes across the ocean. All the nice English homes in Canada, she learned, were already filled. But the Board lady said she'd received a letter from someone named Miss Clementine Pope. The woman was a public health nurse from a far-away part of the world called New Mexico. And she wished to take in a child. Were we interested?

"I'm not sure," said Mother. We were all seated around the table at breakfast. "I don't know any public health nurses."

"I've met dozens of nurses," said Willy. "And they're all splendid."

"A nurse should be able to care for a child," said Father.

"That's true," said Mother. "But she lives in such a faraway place."

"Santa Fe, New Mexico," said Father, who loved maps, globes, atlases and all that sort of thing. "I'm sure I've heard of it."

He jumped up, threw his napkin on the table and strode into the library. Our library was lined from floor to ceiling with books. Willy, Mother and I ran after him and watched as he spun around a large globe.

When he finally put his finger down, I peered at the spot. It seemed nearly on the other side of the world from England! A disagreeable lump swelled in my throat. How could I possibly be forced to travel so far from everything dear to me?

Father, however, seemed pleased. "I daresay the War won't make it all the way over there."

"Why, Beatrice, that's the Wild West," declared Willy gleefully. "Perhaps you'll see cowboys and Indians."

"Oh dear," Mother gasped. "Not cowboys and Indians."

"Honestly, if I must leave home," I said, stamping my foot, "why can't I go somewhere in the countryside where you could visit me once in a while?"

My dear father was thin and tall with tortoise shell glasses always perched on his nose. Now he looked especially serious; his glasses slipped further down his nose. Coming close, he put his hand on my shoulder. "Nowhere in Great Britain is safe enough, darling," he said. "Bombs simply don't know the difference between city homes and country homes."

I looked up, tears in my eyes, knowing what he said was true.

All that had happened a week ago. Today was the first time that Great-Aunt Augusta had heard of my journey. Peering through her lorgnette at me, she commanded, "Come over here, Beatrice."

When I obeyed, she grabbed my shoulders and pushed them up straight. "Don't forget, Beatrice, you come from a very long line of Sims going back to the Earl of Duckchester," said Great-Aunt Augusta. "Remember you're made of strong stuff. Be proud of who you are."

I nodded glumly. Ever since I could remember, the Earl of Duckchester had glared down at me from his portrait hanging in the hall. Truly, I couldn't imagine doing anything good enough to please him, or Great-Aunt Augusta, either.

"Who is accompanying Beatrice on this perilous journey?" asked my great-aunt.

Mother looked uneasy. Father cleared his throat loudly. "Well, uh, we're not quite sure," he muttered.

I brightened momentarily. Mother and Father had wanted

4

Cook's sister, Miss Frimby, a thin, sour woman, to travel with me. But, at the last moment, Miss Frimby got herself engaged to a Navy sailor named Orlando Stiff. She packed up her cardboard suitcase and trotted out the door without even saying a proper "farewell" to anyone in the house. That's the sort of romance that happens during a war, said Father. I hoped the surprising event might delay or even cancel my trip. But that didn't happen.

"My goodness, you can't send her alone, can you?" Great-Aunt Augusta looked shocked.

"I'm afraid we may have to." Father frowned. "The chance of getting a ticket on another ship is too risky." He winked at me. "You can go it on your own, can't you, Toodles?"

I tried to smile. Toodles was a nickname he hadn't used since I was ten.

Mother, however, looked pale. "She is just a child."

"I am not a child," I protested.

"Of course you're not," said Father. "In any case, Beatrice will be traveling first-class. She'll be very comfortable." He turned away slightly and again cleared his throat. "I see no problem whatsoever."

Mother appeared somewhat relieved. "Thank heaven you're so tall for twelve years old, Beatrice. You appear much older."

I frowned. Indeed I was tall, but also gawky, pale and thin with straight-as-a-pin yellow hair. None of Mother's lovely looks – wavy brown hair and dark eyes like a Christmas card Madonna, as Father always said – had settled on me.

"On the bright side, Beatrice, just think – you won't need a smelly gas mask in the States," said Willy.

"But I don't want to go," I mumbled. "I want to stay here

5

and help like you and all the others." By then, however, everyone was busy talking about the new Prime Minister, Mr. Winston Churchill. Would he be able to keep our country strong and safe?

"He certainly has rallied the spirit of the British people," said Great-Aunt Augusta. "Don't you think?"

Later that evening, I made one last protest, cornering Father in the library where he sat reading the newspaper. "You are forcing me against my will," I said. "You are staying here and so are Mother and Willy. Only I have to leave. It's not fair."

"Yes, Beatrice, I know it's not fair." His face grew very sober. "But we have to think of the future, my dear. What if the Nazis succeed?"

"They c-can't possibly," I stammered. "Can they?"

"We certainly hope not. And we're working day and night at the War Office to prevent that from happening. But…" He pointed to the newspaper. "The news is not very good." Father shook his head. "If the worst should come to pass…I couldn't bear to have a child of mine or any English child brought up under the cruel form of government in Germany at present."

I fell silent, feeling the awful weight of his words.

Then Father's face brightened. "Now, Beatrice, you don't have to think of this trip as such a terrible thing. Look at it as an adventure."

"An adventure?" Being torn from my family and everything near and dear to me didn't seem like a very fine adventure.

"There have been loads of Englishwomen who have had adventures in the wildest, most remote places on earth." Father leapt to his feet and began searching among the books on the shelves. "Somewhere I have a book about Gertrude Bell. She

6

traveled across the Arabian desert on horseback." He pulled out a book. "And here's one on Mary Kingsley, another great explorer. She traipsed across Africa wearing a long dress. Once her many layers of petticoats saved her life when she fell into a lion's trap filled with spears."

A lion's trap? Now that did sound interesting, I thought, taking the book.

Father went to his desk. "Let's see, what do explorers need? If you're going to be an explorer, you must take careful notes of everything you see." He pulled open a drawer and shuffled around a bit. "How would you like this?" He held up a little red-leather bound book.

"Keep it with you at all times," he said, handing it to me. "I expect you to fill it with very interesting information."

I took the little red notebook and turned it over in my hand. The leather was smooth and soft. It looked lovely. I hugged Father around the neck. "You are so sweet to give this to me," I exclaimed, wiping away a tiny tear from the corner of my eye. "But I still don't understand how a very ordinary twelve-year-old girl like me can become a world explorer."

"Why not, Beatrice?" Father said.

"But I've rarely even been out of the city," I said. "And then only for outings in the countryside."

"Nevertheless," said Father, sitting down and picking up his newspaper, "I see many great adventures ahead of you."

Though still doubtful, I tucked the heavy book about Mary Kingsley under my arm. I would read a few chapters before leaving. And I would try my very best to make this awful trip into an adventure.

On the day of my departure, 14 September, the rain poured down in sheets, soaking the city. London seemed particularly grey and dismal, coated with wet soot and ashes.

Father said farewell in the morning before leaving for work. He looked sadder and more serious than I had ever seen him. His final words were, "Beatrice, you will undoubtedly encounter many things you have never encountered before." He paused thoughtfully. "But that's a very good thing, really." Then he gave me a long hug. "Be brave, my dearest girl." His voice was scratchy. "I must rush off now to the War Office." Just as he was climbing into a cab, however, he turned back for an instant. "Be sure and keep your notebook handy."

I didn't leave until that evening. Cook and a chambermaid stood in the foyer to say goodbye. Cook, who had known me since I was a tiny baby, hugged me. The new chambermaid, her blond braids tucked under a little white cap, curtsied. I gave a final desperate squeeze to Alfie, my dear little dog. He was a York-shire Terrier with long golden hair that fell in his eyes and a sweet little tail that stuck straight up.

"Be brave," I whispered in Alfie's furry ear and kissed his tiny cold nose. A tear dripped on his silky coat.

Henry, the chauffeur, loaded my trunk into the Bentley, our shiny black limousine. As Willy, Mother and I were driven to the train station, I pressed my forehead to the cool glass and stared out. It was a dark night. Due to the blackout, automobile head-lights couldn't be turned on and there wasn't another trace of light. Every window had been covered with heavy black paper. No one could even smoke a cigarette outside because that tiny glimmer of light might aid a Nazi airman far above. They might see where to drop their accursed bombs.

Still, even in the dark, I knew these streets so well I could imagine the tall stone and brick buildings on either side, so solid and friendly. Would any of them still be standing when I returned? Or would they all have tumbled down in a pile of dust and rubble?

Suddenly, our automobile jolted, throwing us all forward in a heap. "Sorry, M'um," said Henry, "but the street's torn up bad with holes nearly as big as the kitchen stove."

"Don't worry, Henry, I know you're doing the best you can," Mother said. She sat on the edge of the green velveteen seat grasping my hand. Her pointy red nails dug into my palm but I didn't complain. I knew she was nervous and upset.

"I just hope the fighting lasts long enough for me to join up," said Willy. Unlike Father, Mother and me, he was big, strong and athletic, with a ruddy pink face and curly blond hair.

"Please, don't wish that," said Mother. "I couldn't bear it."

"I wish I could join up, too," I exclaimed.

"Oh, darling," Mother moaned.

"What could you possibly do?" asked Willy.

"Nurse the wounded," I quickly responded.

"Nurse the wounded? You're still bandaging your dollies, aren't you?" Willy always picked times like this to act beastly.

I tried to punch him but Mother pleaded, "Please, children, we have a very short time left to be together. Let's be nice to one another." Indeed, at that moment, we reached Victoria Station. The train station, always busy, was now in shambles. Thousands of people, old and young, were frantically trying to leave London.

After one look at the crowd, Mother sank back in the seat. "I can't go any farther. I'm simply too overcome with emotion." Kissing me on the cheek, she begged me, "Please, darling, let's not make a scene. Just pretend you're going away on holiday." For her sake, I held back my sniffles. Mother was a frail person with "weak nerves," as Father said.

"Really, darling," she went on, "this wretched business can't last very long. You'll probably be home for Christmas." She squeezed my hand as I climbed out of the limousine.

Thank goodness Willy finally stopped acting like a pig and started acting like my very dear big brother again. "Don't worry, Beatrice, I'll accompany you to the train with Henry." He helped Henry fetch my large red traveling trunk. Mother waved goodbye through the limousine window, but the glass fogged up so quickly her face was soon a blur.

"Come on, dearie," Henry gestured and hoisted my heavy trunk onto his wide shoulders. I reluctantly followed, staying close behind him and Willy as we burrowed our way through the crowd of desperate people.

On the train platform, I spied a mother giving last minute instructions to her four youngsters, two boys and two girls. "Now, Lucy, you are all heading for an old house in the country," she said, wiping a smudge from the face of the youngest, a small blond girl. "Be very patient with your great-uncle. He's not accustomed to children."

The girl named Lucy smiled brightly, "Of course we will, Mummy. We'll be very, very good." Her mother gave her a big hug.

"How fortunate those children are," I muttered to Willy.

"There are four of them, which is far more cheerful than just being one. And they're staying in England." He nodded but it was too hard to speak in the crowd with the noise of train whistles and people shouting all around.

By staying in England, those children would know all the customs and manners. What was the right thing to do and say and how to use a butter knife and a finger bowl. Where I was going, I knew none of the manners. Or even if the people who lived in that faraway land of New Mexico had any proper manners at all.

The three of us squeezed through the mass of people until we reached the platform for departing trains. We found the one I was supposed to ride on. Seeing the train made me realize that in a few minutes I would truly be on my own. Alone. My knees felt so weak I wasn't certain they'd keep holding me up.

I gasped, "Who will watch over Alfie? What if no one carries him to the air raid shelter at night? What if he escapes and goes looking for me in the fire and smoke?"

"Don't worry, Beatrice, I'll look after Alfie!" Willy exclaimed. "And I'll look after Father, Mother, our home and all of London. Everything will be fine when you return." He gave me a hard, quick squeeze. "I know this feels bloody awful, Beatrice, but you're a kicker, you'll survive."

I nodded and felt in the pocket of my wool jacket for the little red notebook Father had given me. Its soft smooth leather was comforting.

"And write, Beatrice, don't forget to write. Often as you like," Willy added.

"If you'll write back, I will." I said.

Henry helped me up the steep step onto the train. "You'll do fine, luv," he muttered. "I don't know much about New Mexico, but I've heard Mexico is a very jolly place. Very jolly!"

He loaded my trunk into a first-class compartment which, I noticed, was not filled with first-class people. Some were wearing dingy clothes. The air was thick and warm and smelled like stewed prunes. But I had no choice; this was my seat. Fitting myself between a large old lady clutching a brown paper bag and a thin ill-looking woman with a sharp pointed nose, I recalled Cook's remark, "The war is causing everyone hardships, even the better class of people."

At the last minute, a tall, grubby boy popped into the compartment and squeezed down opposite me, though it was easy to see there wasn't an inch of extra space. I looked at him indignantly, but he just glared back. Sneering at my fine clothes, shiny shoes and white gloves, he jabbered, "Whatcha' think this is, ducky, Buckingham Palace?"

The train jolted into motion. I caught one last glimpse of Willy and Henry, wildly waving. Then they were gone. The grubby boy was still staring. My lower lip began to quiver; I bit it hard, squeezing both hands into tight fists. That horrid boy will not see me cry, I thought. Not for all the tea in China.

Chapter Two

A crowded smelly train coach is a dreadful way to begin a trip. Hours later, I walked up the gangplank of the Duchess of York, a ship bound for the United States. I hoped it would be a vast improvement on the train.

Naturally, Father had booked me a first-class stateroom. So I was extremely surprised to open the door of No.14 and see three small boys seated on one of the bunks. Their clothes were ragged and their hair looked like it hadn't been trimmed for months. They scratched their heads as if – oh my God – they might have lice!

The three were chattering to one another in French. But when I walked in, they stopped and stared. Who were they? What were they doing in my stateroom?

I started to shout, "*Allez-vous-en, allez-vous-en!*" That's how my French tutor, Madame Dépeche, addressed Alfie when he was being a pest. It means, "Go away, go away!!"

Instead I turned around and marched down the corridor to the ship's steward. Looking bored, he referred me to the ship's captain, a surprisingly young and rather handsome gentleman in uniform. I stood patiently a moment until he turned in my direction.

"Hullo. I'm Captain Wingate," he said, "Is there a problem, young lady?"

"Excuse me, sir," I said. "But does this ticket mention my sharing my stateroom with anyone?"

He studied the piece of paper. "You're Beatrice Agatha Sims?" I nodded primly. "Yes, I was intending to look in on you," he told me, smiling. "Quite bold for you to be traveling on your own like this. And I'm terribly sorry, Miss Sims, for the inconvenience. But we've had to squeeze a few extra passengers on board wherever we had an extra berth. These children are Jewish orphans from Belgium traveling to relatives in the United States."

I started to complain about their being put in my stateroom. But before I could speak two words, Captain Wingate shook his head sadly. "If only you had seen the pitiful ones left behind because they had nowhere to go."

I walked slowly back to the stateroom. I knew the Jews in Europe were having a very bad time. That's one more good reason, Father said, why England must stand strong against the Nazis. But still – three strange boys in my cabin?

That night I did insist they leave for ten minutes while I dressed for bed. I hated for anyone, even a child, to see me in my cotton slip. So I quite pushed them out the door and jumped

14

under the covers. Then I called out, giving them permission to return. I watched as they crowded noisily into the remaining bunk bed.

A day later, feeling bored, I came across the little red notebook in my jacket pocket. The pages were empty and white. There were no straight lines like on school notebook paper. I could write anything I wanted. Or even draw little pictures. But what to write? I had no idea. Yet if I didn't begin now, I might never. Then I'd return to England in a few months with an empty notebook. Father would be very disappointed. I definitely needed to begin…

I thought for a moment or two. I must pretend to behave like an explorer, even if I didn't feel like one at all. What did explorers think about? What did they write about? For a few seconds my mind went completely blank. Then I considered what an explorer like Mary Kingsley might write about. I had read enough of her book to know she wrote about the people she met on her journeys in Africa. She described them very carefully. So I sat down and wrote:

16 September 1940 - Duchess of York
My three Belgian cabin-mates are small and pale. The only clothes they have is what they're wearing - thin sweaters, shirts and trousers. Also, I hate to say this, but they have the most atrocious table manners I've ever seen. The steward in the dining room seats us at the same table since we come from the same stateroom. The little boys stuff food into their mouths as if they haven't eaten for months!!

I put down my pen, thinking. Perhaps the boys haven't eaten for months. Writing these few lines made me realize how little I knew about these children. They probably had had a terrible time of it. They may have lost their families – why, they were even more alone than me.

When we next dined together, the boys' table manners didn't bother me nearly as much. In fact, watching them eat, my heart went out to them. I took my apple and carefully cut it into thirds, passing a piece to each boy. They hesitated only a second before accepting and eating their apple slices. For the rest of the voyage, I passed them anything I could spare – fruit, bread, cheese. They always gobbled it down in seconds.

In the stateroom, I still ignored them totally. Then four nights into the voyage, the ship sailed into an awful storm. The waves pitched the ship back and forth violently. My stomach did the same – rocking up and down, back and forth. I felt so horribly ill, I must have turned quite white. The three orphans sat on the opposite bunk, watching me with big frightened eyes. Finally I collapsed on the bed, groaning loudly and holding my stomach. That's when the oldest boy came hesitantly over. He sat on the edge of the bed, wiping my forehead with a damp cloth. He even hummed a sweet lullaby he must have learned from his mother. Through that long, turbulent night, he sat close, keeping me company. While on the other bunk, his two little brothers clung to one another fearfully.

Next morning, I lay in bed a long while, feeling grumpy. I was mortified at my behavior. After all, here was a shabbily dressed young boy (with no table manners) who had behaved far better to me than I had behaved toward him.

16

Later that morning he arrived with a cup of weak tea for me. I sat straight up and asked his name. "*Comment appellez vous?*"

He put down the tea, smiled grandly and bowed. "*Je m'appelle Alphonse.*" Then he introduced his little brothers as André and Alfred; they also bowed politely.

Still smiling, Alphonse asked if I would like to play checkers.

"*Oui, oui,*" I replied. For the remainder of the trip, we got along very well, often playing checkers or dominoes in the ship's lounge. They played so brilliantly, however, I lost nearly every game.

A few days later, late at night, the ship docked. The moment I awoke, I could feel the ship's engines had stopped and we were no longer moving through the waves. I jumped up, hastily dressed and ran up on deck, the little boys fast behind me. I couldn't wait to see the Statue of Liberty and giant skyscrapers of New York harbour.

But when I reached the deck of our ship, there was neither a huge statue nor tall, tall buildings.

"This is Norfolk, Virginia," explained Captain Wingate, standing nearby and noticing our disappointment. "We had to zigzag across the ocean to outwit deadly German U-boats. That's why we ended up here instead of in New York."

What a disappointment. Like all British children traveling to the United States, I'd been given a booklet called *The Token of Freedom*. The booklet reassured English children about leaving their homes and families. It helped them understand why Britain was standing fast against the Nazi threat. I read the booklet over and over and kept it under my pillow at night. One paragraph I had memorized:

> *"When you see the Statue of Liberty in New York's harbour, remember why she is holding up a light. It is what any brave mother would do if her children were traveling a dangerous road in what Chaucer called 'the dark darknesses' of this world. The spirit of freedom is so dear to the Free People that they made her image enormous, strong as bronze, beautiful as a proud young mother."*

What stirring words those were! I wished I spoke French well enough to tell Alphonse and his brothers how the "dark darknesses" were spreading in the world. But that brave, free people would always fight against them.

The English were now in the battle and Father believed the Americans would soon join them. "The English and the Americans have been strong allies before and shall be again," he had predicted.

But now we were in Virginia, not New York. Even at the end of September, the weather was sticky and hot. Flowering bushes bloomed like June in England. All the passengers filed off the ship in an orderly fashion. I stood next to my trunk, dressed in long woolen socks and a grey wool argyle sweater over my blouse. In a few minutes, the cotton blouse was damp with sweat.

Alphonse, André and Alfred stood next to me on the dock. Alphonse was quickly learning English. "Wanna play checkers?" he asked.

I shook my head. "No, thank you. Not now."

At that moment, an old couple appeared. Seeing the boys,

they shouted with happiness. Then hurrying over, they hugged the children with tears flowing down their wrinkled faces. Before leaving, the boys crowded round me. Each one kissed me on both cheeks. "*Au revoir, au revoir. Bonne chance.*" Then the family walked away, hand-in-hand, chattering to one another. Looking after them, I pulled out my little notebook and jotted down a few words.

> 21 September 1940 – Norfolk, Virginia
> The refugee children, Alphonse, Andre and Alfred, now have a safe home and will be well-fed. I am very glad I am not a refugee. I am a visitor and a sort of explorer, which is very different.
> I am seeing real Americans for the first time. There are many tall young men in blue and white Navy uniforms. (Their uniforms are mostly white with blue trim while British uniforms are mostly blue with white trim.) I can only hope these sailors will soon be crossing the ocean to aid England in winning the war.

I had barely put away my notebook when the handsome Captain Wingate strolled over. He patted my shoulder. "You still have quite a long trip ahead of you, dear girl."

I frowned. That was not what I wanted to hear. I felt I had traveled quite long enough and I wished simply to be somewhere. Alphonse, Andre and Alfred already had a home, why couldn't I?

Captain Wingate must have noticed me drooping. He quickly

added, "Miss Sims, would you care for an Eskimo Pie?"

"An Eskimo what?"

Captain Wingate marched over to a short plump man behind a little white pushcart. He gave the man a few coins and returned with a square of frozen vanilla ice cream covered in chocolate, on a stick. I quickly learned how delicious Eskimo Pies are! Though the heat caused the ice cream to drip on my sweater and skirt. My fingers became very sticky too. Captain Wingate pulled out his clean white handkerchief to clean up the stickiness. Then he hailed a taxicab to carry me to the train station. Finally, he handed me a thick envelope. Wishing me a good journey, he rushed back to his ship.

Inside the envelope, I discovered a train ticket and a cable from home. How lovely! I tore open the cable.

```
21 September 1940
Dear Sis,
    By now we believe you have reached
dry land. Very lucky your ship didn't
get torpedoed. There was one boat, the
City of Benares, that went down several
days ago and 77 children were drowned.
Those poor little blokes didn't have a
chance. It was a terrible tragedy and
the whole country is mourning. Now Brit-
ain won't send any more children to the
United States so you got out in the nick
of time. Your ship was one of the very
last to make the dangerous crossing. Of
course, Mother says now if she'd known
how dangerous the journey was, she'd
never have permitted you to go. But it's
hardly safe here, either. If anything,
```

```
the bombing is worse than before, so
we're glad you've reached the States.
We all feel much happier knowing you're
safe.
            Fondly,
            William M. Sims a.k.a. Willy
            Home Guard Officer
```

My hands trembled as I folded up the cable and put it in my pocket. Horrors! What if our ship had been hit by torpedoes? Imagine sinking into the freezing cold water! Imagine sharks snapping off my feet! A shiver ran clear through me. The mere sight of Willy's name on the thin blue paper made my eyes brim with tears. "Oh, dear," I murmured.

"Wha-at's tha' you say'd, little la-dy?" asked the big red-faced cabdriver, turning round to stare at me. I could barely understand his drawl. Did all Americans speak in such a peculiar way?

"Nothing." I quickly wiped a tear away with the wadded-up handkerchief from kind Captain Wingate that I had forgotten to return. Then I sat up straight. After all, my journey was far from over. In fact, like it or not, my American adventure was just beginning.

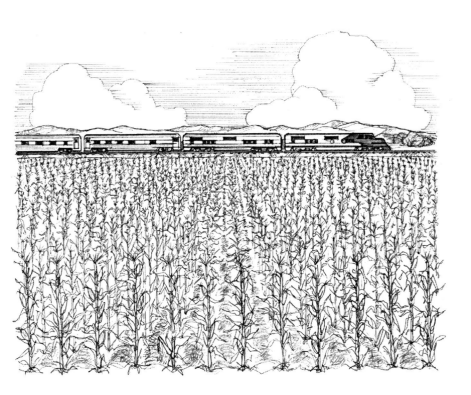

Chapter Three

At first, it was pleasant not to be tossing back and forth on the ocean waves.

The train whizzed past woods, meadows, gardens, orchards, farmhouses, barns and cows. Then more of the same and even more of the same. Someone should make a law, I decided, forbidding countries to be so big. England is the perfect size for a country – no countries need be any larger than that.

I wished I had some friends to play checkers and dominoes with in the train lounge. I missed Alphonse, André and Alfred. What were they doing now? Eating everything in sight? Playing hide and seek in their new home? Did they have a dog or cat to play with? Were they making friends?

23

I stared out the window some more, watching whole towns pass by. Streets with street lamps and telephone poles, houses, lawns, men mowing the grass, women hanging up laundry. Young boys and girls stopped their bicycles on the roadway and waved at the passing train. I waved back, wondering if they saw me. We also passed forests and rivers. Once I spied a deer grazing in a meadow. Another time, a red fox ran close to the train tracks, pausing and looking up as the noisy train passed.

I got out my little red notebook and wrote:

22 September 1940
It's quite remarkable how things in the train compartment fit together so neatly. There's a small white porcelain basin with a mirror above. The water faucets turn off and on, hot and cold. Next to it is a narrow closet with four hangers inside. I hung up three white blouses, a checked skirt and a blue dress. During the day, I sit on a wide flat seat that folds into a comfortable bed at night, with very clean white sheets, a warm blanket and thick pillow. The motion of the train rocks me to sleep. I dream of small towns, forests, meadows and cornfields flashing by in the dark.

Two days later, I changed trains in St. Louis. Soon after that, as I gazed out the window, everything became a monotonous blur. Endless fields of crops with only a few lonely farmhouses scattered here and there. Nothing looked cazy and familiar. I had truly arrived in a strange and different land; remote from everything

I knew and loved. Indeed, how little I knew about the United States. Before coming, Father had told me the country was filled with immigrants.

"What do you mean?" I had asked.

"Most Englishmen have lived in Britain all their lives," said Father. "So did their parents, their grandparents, their great-grandparents and all their ancestors dating back to William the Conqueror."

"But that's not true in the United States?"

"No, Beatrice. In the United States, most people arrived a fairly short time ago. The Indians have always lived there of course. But everyone else came ten years ago, fifty years ago, one or two hundred years ago," he explained. "Some immigrated from England while others came from France or Germany or Italy. There are even immigrants who came from faraway lands like China and Turkey."

Imagining all those people – Germans, Turks, Chinese – heaped together in one place made me feel quite dizzy. I was accustomed to people who looked, sounded and behaved more or less like me. Indeed, my jaw nearly dropped open when I first answered a knock on the train compartment door. Cracking open the door, I saw a tall man in a neat white jacket and dark cap. His round face was dark as coffee; his short grey hair was fuzzy as lamb's wool.

"Excuse me, Miss Beatrice," the tall man said. "I see your name on the top of my list of passengers. I'm Hamilton, porter for this here Pullman car. It's my responsibility that you get looked after, good as can be."

He glanced around the compartment. "You honest-to-God

travelin' on your own?"

I nodded, still too stunned to speak. Hamilton didn't seem to mind; he shook his head. "Ain't you Brits something!" And gave me an admiring look. "Perhaps you'd like me to fetch you a bite to eat from the dining car." He considered. "How about a nice cold Coca Cola with ice, Miss Beatrice?"

"A Coca…what?" I muttered, finally finding my voice.

"Just you wait and see," he replied. Minutes later, he returned with a tray on which I spied a bottle of dark fizzy liquid and a glass filled with ice. He carefully poured the drink into the glass and waited a moment while I tasted it. The sweet bubbly drink sizzled on my tongue. I couldn't help but smile. Hamilton grinned.

"How about a hot dog with mustard and relish?" he inquired next.

"What kind of a dog?" I asked.

He chuckled. "On the menu it says a frankfurter, but most folks here in America call it a hot dog or Coney Island dog."

He brought me one, dripping with all the "fixings" – ketchup, mustard, relish. With such delicious goodies to sample, I certainly didn't lose any weight on the trip.

24 September 1940
Dear Willy,
You may think I'm a little piggy because of how much I'm eating. Especially when people in England are doing without in order that the soldiers can have enough. You are probably still very short on sugar and butter and eggs. But here there's plenty

- we dine on ice cream and grilled cheese toast and sweet bubbly soda pops. Hamilton, the porter, who's a very kind person, makes sure that I have the best of everything. Not that I wouldn't give up any of this delicious food to be with you and Mummy and Father and Alfie. But at least I'm not starving on top of the misery of being here without you.

Sincerely,

Beatrice

The next afternoon, I gathered courage and decided to explore the entire train. It was very long – eighteen cars. Passing through the dining car, I saw several passengers loudly arguing and paused to listen to what they were saying.

A bulky man in a grey suit yelled, "We don't have any business getting involved in this fight. Those countries over there in Europe should have learned their lesson the last time we bailed 'em out!"

A blonde woman with thick red lipstick and rouge agreed. She pointed to her husband, who was a short mousy fellow with a mustache. "I wouldn't want George fighting, anyway. He's already done his part for Uncle Sam." And she added loudly, "Besides, who would he fight for? I've got German relatives myself and so do lots of other red-blooded Americans!"

I couldn't bear hearing another word. "What do you mean?" I burst out, glaring at the woman. "England didn't start this war. England is just trying to keep our people safe from those bullies, the Nazis." My lower lip started to tremble. "This horrid war is all their fault!"

The woman and her friends stared at me. Her husband George said to me, "Sure, sweetie, I can see how you feel that way."

I hated him calling me "sweetie" and looking at me with such pity! Hot tears welled up in my eyes and I raced out of the dining car. How could they talk like that? I had assumed all Americans would want to fight on the side of England. That's what Father believed. Yet now it appeared there were Americans who wanted to fight on the side against England! What a horrid, terrible thought!

I rushed from one car to the next through the train, seeing nothing. Finally reaching my compartment, I sank down onto the seat and blinked back the tears. I forced myself to gaze out the window, though now the scenery sped by in a blur.

A moment later, Hamilton came by. Normally I was pleased to see him, but not this day. "What's the matter, honey?" he said. "Feeling homesick?"

I didn't reply right away. Finally I asked, "Who is Uncle Sam?"

Hamilton chuckled. "Uncle Sam is just a way of talking about the government of the United States. Like the King of England, only the king's a real person, they say, and Uncle Sam ain't real."

"Don't people in America want to fight for England? Don't they know England needs their help?"

"The truth is there's some do and some don't. It's a big question right now," he said. "What to do about this dang war over there in your country." He looked at me so kindly, I wanted to cry again. "Ain't no easy answer."

I turned away from him toward the window. How could anyone say that the answer wasn't easy? The United States had to join the war on the side of England. Didn't they know what would happen if they didn't?

"Can't I get you something, Miss Beatrice?" asked Hamilton, still trying to cheer me up. "How about a nice cream cheese and olive sandwich?"

"No, thank you, Hamilton, not now." Truly, my stomach felt like it was filled with stones. Nothing appealed to me, nothing at all.

"Well, you let me know, honey, if there's anything I can do," said Hamilton, and he quietly closed the compartment door.

I gazed out the window, unseeing, for a few minutes. Then I began to notice what was out there or rather what was not out there. No trees or grass or water. Instead, for miles in all directions, the land was dry, rocky and flat. There were no towns or people or houses. Just a few pathetic-looking cows with horns wide as bicycle handles.

Before leaving, Father had shown me a map of the entire country with various train routes. We'd been riding for almost four days – where were we now? In Kansas, Iowa or Colorado? I was no longer sure.

Oh, how I missed London – its hustle and bustle – horns blaring and people chatting with one another; trams and taxicabs hurtling past and friendly old buildings lining each street. Why, I even missed the patchy grey fog and shiny puddles of rain on every street corner. What I didn't miss was the war – the scream-ing bombs, the black-outs and all that horrid stuff. Yet, surely, the war must be ended by now. Surely, England had beaten back its enemy and peace had returned.

Leaning back on the seat, I closed my teary eyes and dreamt of being home. Of sitting in front of a warm fire crackling in the parlor grate and smelling a smooth custard that Cook is preparing in the kitchen. My adorable pup Alfie is chasing his tail in circles at my feet and then and then—

Suddenly Hamilton's booming voice rang out. "Next stop Lamy. Lamy, New Mexico, next stop." A moment later, he knocked at the compartment door. "This is your destination, Miss Beatrice. Says so on your ticket. I'll go fetch your trunk, soon as you're ready to go."

My stomach dove to my toes. Oh dear, oh dear, oh dear! In a few minutes, I would meet Miss Pope. What would she look like? What would she think of me? I jumped up and stood in front of the mirror for a moment. Was I dressed well enough? Would I make a good impression? No indeed, I wasn't presentable at all.

Rushing about, I changed into a crisp peacock blue dress, a pair of shiny black patent dress shoes, white cotton gloves, a light coat and bouncy little hat. Gazing again into the mirror, I turned this way and that, inspecting every inch of my outfit. Now I looked like a proper English girl from a good family. No one could complain about my appearance, not even Great-Aunt Augusta.

Hamilton set my trunk near the exit door as the train slowed down, brakes screeching loudly. A small group of people waited to disembark, chatting merrily with one another, all eager to arrive. I seemed to be the only one not pleased and excited. I wished the train would start rolling in the opposite direction. I wished it would carry me all the way back across the United States to the

Atlantic Ocean. From there, I could jump on a ship – even if I needed to hide in the cargo – that would sail back to England and home.

Instead, the train screeched to a stop. Giggling, everyone grabbed something to hold onto, even one another. A tiny old lady gripped my shoulder. "Excuse me, dearie," she murmured.

"You wait for me, Miss Beatrice," Hamilton called from the corridor behind us. After all the other passengers scrambled off, he swung my trunk down to the platform. I tried to follow. Instead of putting my foot down firmly on the step, however, my eyes were dazzled by hot intense sunlight. I almost pitched headfirst onto the platform.

Fortunately, Hamilton put out his hand in the nick of time and lifted me down. "Goodness gracious, Miss Beatrice," he exclaimed, "here you've come to the end of a long dangerous trip and you nearly hurt yourself bad!"

Standing next to my trunk, I gazed around. Oh, but what a dreadful place I'd come to! There was nothing here but a pathetic little train station, an old hotel and a short dirt road. Two small children with skin the color of wet tea leaves played in the dusty road. Glancing up, they stared as if I were extremely curious-looking, then muttered to one another in a language that was not English.

"Are you quite sure, Hamilton, we are still in the United States?" I asked.

"Yes'm, we are," replied Hamilton with a smile.

I looked closer at the dark-haired children. "What language do they speak?"

He chuckled, "I s'pose they speak Spanish."

"Spanish!" I exclaimed. "Why do they speak Spanish?" Just at that moment the train-whistle sounded loudly.

"I've got to be on my way, Miss Beatrice." Hamilton gave me a kind look and quickly stepped back on the train. "Whoever's coming to pick you up will be here shortly. I'm sure of that." He waved. "And don't you worry, soon you'll be in your new American home."

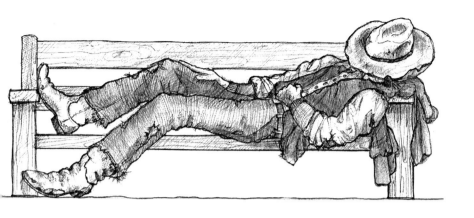

Chapter Four

By the time the train rounded a bend and disappeared from sight, I already missed Hamilton and my snug little train compartment. What was I doing in this strange place?

The train platform was filled with passengers and their baggage, at first. Very quickly, however, people grabbed their suitcases, hatboxes and valises and departed. Soon there was no one but me. Or so I thought. Then I glanced around and saw a skinny old fellow stretched out on a bench, fast asleep. I carefully removed my notebook from my coat pocket and began to write:

> 25 September 1940 – Lamy, New Mexico
> I am seeing my first cowboy, I be-
> lieve. At least he looks like the cow-
> boys in Western movies. The ones
> who ride into town and start shooting
> their guns. He's wearing blue dunga-
> rees and he has a big felt hat over his
> face which, I presume, shades him
> from the sun. I could see more if I
> stepped any closer. But I don't dare.

Just as I finished making notes, the cowboy woke up. He yawned, stretched, sat up and plunked his hat down on his head. I hastily put my pen and notebook back in my purse, hoping he hadn't seen me scribbling in it. I turned away and gazed firmly in the other direction. But to my absolute horror, the cowboy sauntered over to me and spoke. "Y'all waiting for somebody?"

His face was rough and wrinkled; his teeth yellow. One cheek bulged out and whatever he was chewing had a foul odor. Suddenly, the most terrifying thought crossed my mind. Had this awful man come to the station to meet me? What if he'd sent the cable to my parents in London pretending to be a respectable woman named Miss Clementine Pope?

Cook often read news stories to me about children kidnapped by ruffians and turned into slaves. Could this be what the old cowboy intended? My eyes widened and I froze.

"Cat got your tongue, little girl?" He grinned, revealing a big gold tooth.

I gulped. "I'm, uh, waiting for my dear Uncle and Auntie. They're always a wee bit late." I craned my neck and peered down the road, hoping to fool him. Whatever happened, I decided, under no circumstances would I go anywhere with this cowboy!

"Hmm, that so?" Contrary to my fearful expectations, he showed no further interest in me. Instead he turned and sauntered over to a skinny brown horse tied to a nearby pole. The horse looked nearly as scruffy as he. Climbing on his sorry steed, the cowboy grinned, waved his hat and yelled, "Yahoo!" Then the two galloped off down the road.

Gracious! Was he waving and yelling at me?

As he galloped from sight, a cloud of dust appeared in the road. A moment later, an old blue truck emerged from the dust and stopped near the train platform. A woman quickly jumped out and strode up to me. From her brisk walk and manner, I guessed she was quite young. But as she came closer, I spied little wrinkles around her eyes and grey streaks in her sandy hair, which was long and pulled back from her wide forehead in a loose bun. She wore no hat at all.

"Beatrice? Beatrice Sims? Golly, I'm mighty sorry to be late. Have you been waiting long?" The woman smiled broadly and stuck out her hand. "My name is Clementine Ophelia Pope but folks around here call me Clem."

I stared in dismay. She was barely an improvement on the old cowboy. Not a bit elegant or fashionable, she wore a checked shirt and long brown trousers. Below the hem of the trousers, I spied boots! Dusty black boots. I had never seen a lady like her before. *A lady?* It was clear to me that Miss Pope was not a lady! At least not the sort of lady I had seen having tea with my mother or Great-Aunt Augusta.

I put forth my hand in its neat white cotton glove and grasped hers gingerly. The grip was firm, like my father's. The skin looked rough with nails cut short and no trace of polish. She certainly wasn't wearing dainty gloves like mine.

Miss Pope gazed at my trunk. "That thing looks heavy as a bale of green hay. Maybe two bales." She turned to me. "But I guess the two of us can manage to tote it to the truck." Her grey eyes were clear as a child's.

My mouth dropped open. "The two of us," I stammered.

Miss Pope glanced around the platform. "Don't see another soul who could help." I already knew there was no one. Miss Pope reached down, grasped the trunk handle and lifted one end. Her arm was taut beneath her neat red and white checked shirt. I leaned over, too, gripping the handle and tugging. But the trunk didn't budge, not even slightly.

"It's awfully heavy!" I gasped.

Miss Pope nodded. "Sure as heck is – what did'ya pack? *The Oxford English Dictionary?*" She chuckled.

I tried to look dignified. "I believe I can do without my things for a few hours. Until you can send somebody 'round for it."

Miss Pope's eyebrows shot up. She repeated my words, "Send somebody 'round for it?" She scratched her head while a smile tugged at the corner of her mouth. "You mean like a…a footman?" She dropped her end of the trunk. "I don't s'pose it would hurt this darn thing to sit here for a while. 'Til a footman shows up." Her smile grew wider. I knew she was joking with me. And I didn't appreciate the insult to my dignity. I pursed my lips and said nothing.

"Sorry, kid," Miss Pope added. "But I'm afraid there's nobody gonna haul that thing outta here but us."

Who was she calling *kid?* My cheeks burned as I reached again for the handle. I tugged and tugged and tugged. Finally, jerking and dragging the heavy old thing a few inches at a time, we managed to get it to the truck. Then after a lot of effort we hoisted it into the back.

Miss Pope patted the truck's fender fondly. "This is my pal, Maude. We've gone quite a few miles together." She winked at me. "Bet you grow to like her, too."

The very idea! I won't be here long enough to grow fond of your horrid old truck, I thought. Or you!

"Okay, Beatrice, hop in and we'll head into town." Hop in? How did one gracefully climb into a truck? I grasped the handle, and jerked open the passenger door. *Cluck, cluck, cluck!* Brown and black feathers flew in my face! I jumped back down as two chickens cackled loudly at me from a crate on the front seat.

Miss Pope burst into laughter. "Sorry, kid, but I was in such a hurry to get here, I forgot about those little biddies." She grabbed the crate and placed it alongside my trunk, still chuckling.

Before sitting down, I carefully inspected the seat for feathers or worse. I didn't want to spoil my clean skirt.

"You see, I was late picking you up," Miss Pope said, climbing in and starting the engine. "Cause I was out at the Rodriguez house, helping Señora Rodriguez give birth." She turned to me with a pleased grin. "And guess what?"

"I'm sure I can't imagine," I replied tartly.

"She had twins. Baby boys. That's why they gave me two chickens instead of one!"

Chapter Five

The truck bumped and jolted out of the dusty lot and onto a narrow dirt road. The land surrounding us was the most desolate I'd ever seen. Bare dirt and rocks. In the distance, I spied a long low spiky ridge that looked like a dinosaur had fallen asleep there a million years ago and been covered with dust. Further away were hills that resembled flat cardboard triangles pasted on the horizon. There was barely any grass or proper trees and bushes, only stubby green things that seemed like a cross between a bush and a tree.

Miss Pope noticed me looking at the stubby things. "Those are piñon trees," she said. "They don't get very tall but the wood's great for burning. And they produce lots of piñon nuts every fall for people to eat."

I bit my lip, thinking of the lovely trees in England – majestic oaks and regal maples, slim beeches and handsome hawthorns.

"Honestly, I don't believe there's any place more beautiful on earth," said Miss Pope, gazing around.

Beautiful? What was beautiful about it? I couldn't imagine.

"Hardly anyone lives here," I observed. Indeed there was not a single house in view. Obviously, most people didn't care for the place as much as Miss Pope.

"You're right about that," she agreed cheerfully. "It's one reason I moved to New Mexico. I tried cities for a while but just never fit in. The West is where I belong."

The Wild West? I remembered what Willy had said. Yes, I was definitely in the Wild West now. And it was truly awful.

Miss Pope reached over and patted my shoulder. "Now London, that's a wonderful city," she said. "So full of culture and history. How terrible to see a place you love being bombed."

I glanced over curiously. "Have you ever been to London?" I couldn't imagine this plain woman in her felt hat and scuffed boots wandering through my city.

"Yes, I was in England many years back," said Miss Pope. She looked a little sad. But before I could ask any more, she added, "The whole world believes you Brits are very brave to stick it out."

"Do you imagine we have a choice?" I exclaimed. "We could never give in to those nasty Nazis!" I thought of Father going to the War Office every day while Willy worked nights to help ambulance drivers. No one in England was going to give up, not ever. I sat up proudly.

Miss Pope glanced over at me with a hint of approval in her

eyes. What a relief that she appeared to be on Britain's side, unlike the American couple on the train.

The truck slowed to a stop. Why? Weren't we still in the middle of nowhere? Then I heard a faint *baa, baa, baa* and peered out. A herd of spindly white sheep blocked the road. Finally, a familiar sight. There are sheep grazing almost everywhere in England, even on London heaths. What a difference, though, between the green of England and the rocky soil now surrounding us. I couldn't imagine what sheep in New Mexico found to eat!

The animals bumped into one another as they sidled along, bleating. Beside them walked a wrinkled old man, waving a cane. Next to him bounded a black and white sheep dog. The old shepherd smiled toothlessly at us, but didn't hurry to get out of our way. Miss Pope didn't seem bothered in the least. She leaned back in her seat, waved and called, "*Buenos Días*."

Finally, we started rolling again. I looked back at the sorry beasts. If they lived in my country, they'd be standing knee-deep in a grassy meadow. English sheep, I decided, simply had no idea how lucky they were!

The truck bumped along for a few more miles. I was growing more and more bored and weary. Then we reached the top of a rise. Straight ahead, I saw mountains – my first real mountains. A flutter passed through my chest. "Oh, my," I gasped.

The mountains were huge and rounded, mighty and gentle at the same time. The sun had dropped lower in the sky, so the hot afternoon glare was gone. The mountain slopes were bathed in warm gold and red rays. In fact, everywhere the air was clear and sparkly. Even the dirt road seemed to glisten.

Miss Pope smiled as if she knew a secret. "That's Santa Fe

ahead," she said.

I strained to look, but could see little in the distance. No tall buildings or church spires. Nothing to signal what was there. For the next twenty minutes, I leaned forward, eager to spy my new home. But when the truck rolled into Santa Fe, I only saw ugly square brown houses, flat on top. The roads in town weren't even paved. They were narrow and dusty as cow paths in the country-side!

My spirits sank. No place on earth seemed more different than my dear London. Why, Santa Fe was as strange and foreign as Bombay or Zanzibar. If Mother had known of the dry barren hills and ugly brown houses, would she have sent me here?

"This is the Santa Fe River," Miss Pope said as we crossed a low bridge. She pointed to a slim trickle of water.

"You're calling *that* a river? That pathetic little stream!" I couldn't contain myself another second. "The Thames is a river!" I declared.

Miss Pope didn't seem offended. "You're right," she said, "we're short on water around here, specially at this time of year. Just wait 'til spring, then you'll see a torrent."

"But I won't be here in the spring," I exclaimed loudly. "By then I shall certainly be home with my family."

Miss Pope's voice was kind. "I hope so, too, Beatrice." Finally stopping in front of a little house, she smiled. "Are you hungry? Dolores has been cooking all day."

The front door swung open and a thin dark woman appeared. She murmured a shy greeting to me as we got out of the truck and then helped Miss Pope drag the trunk inside. She returned to fetch the crate of chickens, muttering fondly to the noisy creatures.

At least there's one servant, I thought, so I won't be expected to do everything. "Come on in, Beatrice." Miss Pope led me to a plain little room, barely larger than the ship's cabin. She gave me a keen look. "Guess you're used to something fancier."

Swallowing my disappointment, I murmured, "It's charming."

"You probably want to wash up," Miss Pope said and departed.

Indeed, I could barely wait to rinse the dust off my shiny black patent leather pumps, off my white silk stockings and dress, off my hands and face. Whew – I felt like Alfie after a tumble in the hearth soot. In the mirror above the sink, I stared at my pale face and grey eyes, ringed with limp straight-as-a-pin yellow hair. For a descendant of the Earl of Duckchester, I was not distinguished-looking. Just the opposite, I doubted if there was a duller-looking girl anywhere. Oh well, I flopped down on the bed – what did it matter? There was no one in this horrid place whom I wanted to impress.

My head sank into the pillow. But barely a moment later Miss Pope yelled, "Time for supper!" She sounded as if she was summoning barn animals to the trough.

I struggled to my feet and followed my nose to the dining room. I hoped there'd be some jolly treats like those on the train. Coney Island dogs and hamburgers on buns with ketchup. But nothing on the table looked familiar. As I sat down, Miss Pope spooned a thick stew of meat and vegetables onto a plate. Then she handed me a round white, very flat thing.

"Have a tortilla," said Miss Pope. "We eat this instead of bread."

My stomach was growling, so I took one bite of the stew and then another. The food was surprisingly tasty. Soon every morsel disappeared. I glanced at Miss Pope's plate, still piled high with a second helping. She certainly didn't believe in lady-like portions. Why, she ate nearly as much as Willy! Miss Pope glanced in my direction. "You sure you got enough to eat? You're mighty skinny for a gal your age."

"Yes, thank you." I daintily wiped my mouth. Then I neatly placed my knife and fork across the plate as I'd been instructed to do at the end of a meal. Miss Pope didn't seem to know that rule either. She mopped her plate with a scrap of tortilla like a scullery maid. Finally, she pushed her chair back from the table and gazed in my direction. "Dolores sure knows how to cook. Don't you agree?"

"I…I suppose it was very good," I mumbled in surprise. No one had ever asked my opinion of a meal. The rule in our house at the dinner table was that children were to be seen and not heard.

"Yes, it was a good meal and good for you, too," said Miss Pope. She gazed at my thin frame and added, "That'll put some meat on your bones." Then she sat back in her chair comfortably. "So now, tell me all about yourself. I want to hear everything. About your family, your school, your friends, your pets, what you do for fun. Don't leave out a thing."

"Excuse me," I stared at her. "You want to know about *me*?" Again, I was unused to personal questions. "There…there isn't very much to tell."

"Oh, sure there is," said Miss Pope. "Here in New Mexico, we're so darned far from the rest of the world, we count on visitors like you to tell us what's going on. Don't hold back – tell me everything."

Miss Pope looked genuinely interested. As if I were Marco Polo returning from distant China with grand tales to tell. But what could I possibly say? I slowly began to speak and gradually the trickle of words turned into a torrent.

"Mother is very elegant," I said. "She loves to entertain or go to the theater or to parties. Father is an extremely dear person, though he doesn't like parties nearly as much as Mother. He prefers being in his library reading and smoking a pipe." My voice grew stronger. "Willy, my brother, is good at every sport: cricket, tennis, rugby. He adores them all. And then there's Alfie – the sweetest little dog you can imagine."

I described summer holidays and weekend excursions. "Father and I love to go to the British Museum to see the Egyptian mummies and Chinese vases and medieval armor."

I added, "Mother and I sometimes attend a matinee at the Old Vic Theater. Once we saw *A Midsummer Night's Dream*. And another time we saw *Peter Pan* – they were extraordinary. In winter, we go Christmas shopping at the big department store, Harrods. And if there's time, we stop for tea at Claridges. Such a lovely old hotel." I sighed, remembering the taste of French petit-fours and fresh lemon tarts.

"Of course, nowadays, nobody goes anywhere," I paused, frowning. "Unless they absolutely have to."

Only a few weeks before, I had passed the movie theater where I had once seen *Heidi*. Now the theater was a gaping hole – inside were rows of green velvet seats, crushed into splinters and covered with plaster dust. Such a terrible sight, so awful to see. All of a sudden, I didn't want to remember any more. Words dried up in my mouth and I fell silent.

Miss Pope seemed to understand. She gazed at me kindly for a moment, then stood up and began gathering dishes from the table. "Dolores goes home soon as she's got dinner on the table. She's got her own family to feed so we do the cleaning up." Miss Pope carried the dishes into the kitchen.

There was that word again – we. I sat still, unsure what to do. In my home in London, there were servants who carried off the dirty plates. I barely knew where they went. For a few moments, I remained seated with my hands folded politely in my lap. I could hear the clink of dishes from the other room. Miss Pope was loudly singing a tune. "*Dinah, won't you blow, Dinah, won't you blow, Dinah, won't you blow your hooo-rn.*"

At last, I couldn't bear sitting doing nothing for another moment. If that's how I behaved for the next few weeks or months, my life would be very dull.

I stood up and walked through a swinging door into the kitchen.

Miss Pope was cheerfully scrubbing plates in the sink. Her hands were covered with foamy white soapsuds. She nodded quickly in my direction and continued singing, "*Dinah, won't you blow...*" I watched her work for a brief moment, then spluttered, "Is...is there anything I can do to...to help?"

"Thought you'd never ask." Miss Pope grabbed a dishtowel and flung it at me. Then she handed me a wet plate. "You can dry," she said, grinning. "You know how, don't you?"

I nodded, stiffly, though I didn't know the first thing about drying dishes. Fortunately, the task is not very difficult and I got the hang of it quickly. I felt rather proud when there was a stack of shining plates and glasses to put away. Miss Pope showed me where everything fit in the cupboards. The kitchen was small but very tidy.

When the housework was finished, she leaned against the counter, looking around the room with satisfaction. "By the time I was your age, I looked after my five younger brothers and sisters. I cooked, cleaned, did the laundry, shopping, everything."

"But where was your mother?" I asked.

"She was sick a lot," Miss Pope replied, "that's how I became a nurse."

"Oh yes, you're a nurse," I said, thinking for a moment. "And you say you started when you were just a girl?"

"I had to 'cause Mom was sick so much," said Miss Pope. "I hated it, at first, changing bedpans and all that stuff." She wrinkled her nose. "But then Mom died when I was fifteen and I needed to do something to earn money. Nursing was all I knew how to do."

I looked at Clem with new admiration. Very few women in our circle worked in any sort of job. Mother stayed very busy, but she certainly wasn't employed in a profession. Nor were any of her friends. And it would be impossible to imagine Great-Aunt Augusta working in a job. Yet Miss Pope was a nurse, a real nurse. Moreover, she had begun working when she was only a few years older than me. Suddenly I was very curious.

"How does one become a nurse?" I asked. "Is it very difficult? What do you do exactly?"

"Hold on there." Miss Pope smiled. "That's a lot of questions and it's getting late. But I'll be happy to tell you another time. Or show you. Nursing has been good for a country girl like me. It's taken me places I never would have gone and I've met lots of swell people." She took a bottle of lotion off a shelf over the sink and began to rub some on her hands, which were rough and slightly red. She glanced at my hands, thin, soft and pale.

"It's funny but when I wrote those folks in London, I thought they'd send a poor little kid with hardly any clothes on her back." She smiled. "Instead, you arrive with that giant trunk of yours."

Miss Pope started walking out of the kitchen. Watching her go, I suddenly felt uneasy. I thought of the Jewish orphans and the old couple who was overjoyed to see them. Running after her, I called out, "Miss Pope – Miss Pope."

She stopped so short, I nearly ran into her. "You know, Beatrice, it's real nice how you call me "Miss Pope," but from now on, please, just call me Clem. That's what people around here call me and what I'm used to."

I gulped. "Yes, *uh,* I will call you Clem, if that's what you prefer."

She gazed at me, her eyes twinkling. "And would you mind very much if I called you "Bea" instead of Beatrice? Beatrice is a very pretty name but out West, we sometimes don't take the time for long names."

I considered a moment. Everyone had always called me Beatrice. Should I insist on keeping the same name? What other things about me were going to change?

"I suppose I wouldn't mind," I declared. "I do like bees. You know, the kind that buzz."

"Yep, I like bees, too," said Clem. "They keep the fruit and the flowers going. Why, we couldn't do without bees." Then she stuck her hands on her hips and looked me squarely in the eye. "Now wasn't there something else you wanted to ask me?"

The words nearly stuck in my throat but finally I murmured, "You…you aren't disappointed, are you? You're not sorry because I'm not the poor little child you thought I would be?"

"Disappointed? Me?" Clem shook her head vigorously. "Every kid deserves to be safe. Every kid in the world. It's just…it's just I wasn't expecting such a little princess!"

Chapter Six

T he next morning I awoke with a jolt. A little princess!
How ridiculous! The very idea that someone could
suggest such a thing! Nothing could be further from my idea of
myself. In my family, I had always been the ugly duckling, not the
swan. It was clear I wasn't as pretty as Mother, strong as Willy or
nice as Father. In fact, I wasn't sure what my best qualities were
or if I had any. I frowned as I looked up at the ceiling in my little
bedroom. Then I sat up and glanced around. Thank goodness, I
shan't be here very long, I thought, fetching my sotebook. So I
should describe what I see...

26 September 1940 - Santa Fe

My room is small and simple. It is painted all white with dark round wooden beams above in the ceiling. The closet door is blue and so are the wide windowsills. Somehow the room looks like a cottage in a fairy tale. Perhaps I am truly living in a fairy tale cottage. In which case I might be a little princess like Miss Pope (Clem) said last night – a princess who was forced to come to this strange foreign country against her will. She is under an evil spell, a spell that she must break in order to become free and return home.

I put down my pen and I read back over my notes. It was a bit shocking to see how my writing ran away from me. I had started with the simple facts of what I saw. But suddenly my imagination seemed to seize the pen and go off in another style – toward fantasy and fairy tales. Certainly that was not how explorers wrote. But was it so very wrong? Would Father be unhappy if I didn't write exactly like an explorer? Surely, there were different sorts of writers, each good in their own way.

As I pondered this matter, Clem's voice rang out. "Dolores, have you got that thermos of coffee? I'm running late."

Was Clem leaving already? So early in the day? I threw aside the covers and jumped out of bed. Then I dug through my trunk for something to wear. Most of the shirts and skirts were mussed and wrinkled. "I must ask Dolores to iron these," I muttered.

Finally I found a red sweater and plaid skirt, decent enough to wear. I dressed and rushed into the hallway. Just in time to see Clem who was standing at the door. She carried a large red thermos in one hand and an old leather satchel in the other. Catching sight of me, she paused. "Hey, Bea, thought you might sleep longer. Figured you'd be tired."

"Where are you going?" I asked, tucking in my blouse and smoothing back my hair. I realized I hadn't even looked at myself in the mirror.

"I'm on my way to a nearby Indian village. There's a few cases of influenza and tuberculosis to deal with. It's a tough trip out there, so I imagine I'll be gone all day."

"You're going all day?" I exclaimed. What would I find to do all day by myself?

"Don't worry, Bea," said Clem. "Dolores will give you something to eat. Then you can head for school."

School? I was so surprised I could barely speak. Besides, Clem had already disappeared through the door and was heading toward Maude. I hadn't imagined attending school in the United States. What if I was only here until Christmas, as Mother had said? Why should I bother with classes and teachers?

I headed into the kitchen. Something smelled quite delicious. Dolores was standing at the stove, frying eggs and potatoes in a big black skillet. She glanced up.

"That Señora Clem, she goes to work early every day. She work all the time." Dolores wrapped a tortilla around some egg and potato, then handed me the neat little package. "Here you go, *mi hita*. You eat this on your way to school. Don't worry, Señora Clem tell the teachers you're coming today. They're looking for you."

"But I have no idea where to go," I said. "I've never even seen this school."

"Esteban will show you."

"Esteban?" I asked.

As if waiting for his cue, a boy walked in the back door. I knew at once he was Dolores' son. He had the same thin serious face, but there was a big difference. While Dolores was not a particularly pretty woman, Esteban was a very handsome boy. So handsome, I nearly dropped my egg-filled tortilla on the floor.

His eyes were dark and grave. A long black lock of hair fell over his forehead. Though thin, he looked strong and quick. Most of the boys I knew were either blond or red-haired. They seemed dull as biscuit dough next to this fellow. Suddenly, school didn't seem like such an awful idea.

Esteban appeared as curious about me as I was about him. I could see him eyeing me as he spoke briefly to his mother in Spanish. She kissed his cheek fondly as she gave him a rolled up tortilla, too. Moments later, the two of us were walking down the sidewalk toward school. We walked stiffly, neither of us saying a word or even glancing at the other. Finally, I gathered the courage to ask, "Do you know English?"

Esteban whirled around, his eyes bright with anger. "I bet I speak it better than you."

That shut me up for a second, but then I retorted, "You think you speak English better than me? I'm from England. We…we invented English."

"I know where you're from," said Esteban. "I've seen your British Spitfires blasting the Nazis." He imitated a gunner manning a machine gun and spraying bullets across the sidewalk. "Bam, bam, bam." He looked at me respectfully. "Your country

– it's in all the newsreels."

I was pleased he thought so well of my countrymen. "Yes, everyone is protecting their homes," I said. I wanted to tell him more, about the underground bomb shelters and the smelly gas masks. But at that moment, we rounded a corner. Ahead was a school with a sign out front – Harrington Junior High School. In the schoolyard were dozens of girls and boys about my age.

Yet there was nothing English about this school. For one thing, the students weren't wearing uniforms. The girls were dressed in dresses and skirts and blouses of every different color and style. The boys also wore whatever they chose. That was another surprise. In England, boys and girls rarely attended the same school. I had never been in a classroom with a boy.

Esteban stopped, seeming uneasy, and turned to me. "Look, uh – you can make it from here on your own – can't you?"

I immediately understood his feelings. He didn't want to be seen with me, a strange girl, at his side. I tried to sound braver than I felt. "Oh, yes, Esteban. Of course I can. You go right ahead."

He started to leave my side, then turned back. "And one more thing. In school, call me Steve. You got that?" he insisted. "Not Esteban, just Steve."

I hesitated a second, then murmured, "Yes, Steve."

He nodded with a lopsided grin, then darted off to join a group of boys. One was throwing a ball to another who held a bat. Their game appeared very similar to the English game of cricket, yet somehow it was also quite different.

I was trying to figure out the difference when a voice interrupted my thoughts. "Steve's kinda' good-looking, isn't he?"

A few feet away stood a chubby girl with curly carrot-colored hair. She had caught me gazing across the schoolyard at Esteban…that is, Steve. We both watched as he reached high with one arm to catch the small white ball.

"He is rather handsome," I admitted.

"Ooh," squealed the carrot-top. "I love the way you say 'rather,' raw-tha handsome. I wish I could say it like that."

I turned to look at this girl. Was she always so silly?

"My name's Arabella," she said quickly. "You must be the English girl who's come to stay with Clem. You know how I know? My uncle, Diego Johnson, told me you were coming. He's Clem's neighbor." She smiled a dimply smile. "Have you met him yet?"

I shook my head. "Oh, no, I've only just arrived."

The girl squealed again. "There you go again! Only just arrived! You speak like Mary Poppins or Christopher Robin," she rattled on. "Those were my favorite children's books. I still keep them on a shelf next to my bed."

I started to reply that I loved those books, too. Plus *Wind in the Willows* and *The Secret Garden* – all English books! But at that moment, the school bell rang loudly and boys and girls began grabbing books and racing for the entrance.

"Let's go," Arabella shouted. She rushed toward the school and I followed, feeling just like Mary's little lamb.

Chapter Seven

I had always found school to be awfully dull. Teachers in England are usually strict. My previous teacher, Miss Grimsby, walked around the classroom with a stern gaze. She didn't hesitate to rap any girl on the knuckles who was daydreaming or gossiping or doing anything except studying her textbook. Anyone who has read books by Charles Dickens knows that British grammar schools are not fun.

I soon discovered American schools were very different. As I slid into the desk next to Arabella, a pretty young woman came over and introduced herself as Mrs. Montoya. When everyone in the class was seated, she said, smiling, "We're so fortunate today. We have a new student." Her smile grew wider. "This is Beatrice

Agatha Sims. She comes from England."

All the students turned and stared. Someone at the back
of the room snickered. My face felt quite hot and I tried to
stare back boldly. If only they knew I was a descendent of Lord
Duckchester, I thought, then they would be respectful. But in the
next instant, I realized that not one person in that entire room
knew or cared who Lord Duckchester was. The thought gave me
a sudden shock. All my life I had been raised to believe that I was
only important because of my family, where we lived, who we
were, who knew us. If I wasn't a Duckchester, who was I? Was I...
just...nobody?

For a second, I felt frozen with fear. Then a startling new
idea emerged. I began to see that if I wasn't a Duckchester, then I
could be...I could be anyone – anyone I chose to be.

"Please, call me Bea," I said, quickly. The teacher nodded.
Arabella grinned. I settled more comfortably into my seat.

Looking around the room, I noticed that half the children
were light brown like Esteban. There was one little girl whose
dark face resembled my dear train porter, Hamilton. Such
very different children all in the same schoolroom! Great-Aunt
Augusta would certainly be scandalized. On the other hand, what
would Mary Kingsley think? For an explorer, this classroom was
far more interesting than one filled with students of all the same
hue and manner.

"Does everyone know where England is?" Mrs. Montoya
asked the class.

Only half the students raised their hands. I wondered if that
meant the other half *didn't* know. Mrs. Montoya put her hand
on the shoulder of a tall blond boy. "Donald, please point out

England for us on the map," she told him, nodding toward a large map of the world that hung in front of the room. Every country was a different color – blue, green, purple, yellow. Donald stood up with a bored look and ambled up to the map. First he put his finger on Portugal.

"No, dummy, England is not purple," said Arabella. "It's pink. And it's an island."

"I would prefer you didn't use the word dummy, Arabella," said Mrs. Montoya in a sweet but firm voice. She looked at me. "Perhaps you'd like to show us where England is, Bea."

Of course I wanted to show them. I wanted them all to know–the ignoramuses! Donald glared at me as I took his place in front of the map. I stared at the different colored nations for a second. It wasn't difficult to locate the tall skinny island that I so loved. But how lonely and faraway it looked. My finger shook slightly as I pointed out my country.

"How many of you know that England is now at war?" asked Mrs. Montoya.

Every hand in the class shot up.

Donald said, "And they're getting the heck bombed out of 'em."

At his words, my knees felt weak and shaky. How could I possibly explain to these stupid girls and boys what it feels like when a bomb explodes nearby? How the earth shakes all around?

"Who knows which country is fighting England?" asked Mrs. Montoya. A few hands moved up. I slid my finger over to a big blue blob in the center of Europe and gulped. Germany looked four times bigger than England.

"Yeah," said Donald. "Germany might hammer England back

to the Dark Ages." Several voices tittered at the back of the class where Esteban sat with his friends from the schoolyard.

"Donald, that's not very nice," Mrs. Montoya began to say.

"Oh, it's much worse than that," I interrupted, anger fueling my voice. "Just look." My finger began dotting nearly all the nations of Europe. "Poland and Belgium and Holland and Denmark and France." I turned to the class. "They have all been invaded by the beastly Nazis. Only my dear little England remains free." I gazed earnestly at the students at their desks. "And who's going to help her? Is your giant country, the United States, going to come to our aid?" There was an awkward pause while the students stared at me. Even Donald sat silent.

"Thank you, Beatrice," said Mrs. Montoya. "I believe we all learned a lot just now."

Returning to my desk, my cheeks felt hot and my eyes smarted with tears. Arabella smiled at me, but I couldn't even look in her direction. A little later, Mrs. Montoya came up to my desk. "I know it's very hard, *mi hita*," she said, "We are praying for your country."

That first day of school passed so quickly, I was surprised when the final bell rang. The only major disappointment was lunch. We stood in a line with trays and dinky silverware and were served rather soggy meat and vegetables. Like what you might receive in England if you ate in a not-very-first-rate restaurant or pub.

It was a pleasure, however, to see ample milk, butter and sugar on the table. And since it's always pleasant to have tea with plenty of milk and sugar, I asked for a cup. That surprised everyone.

"How old are you?" asked Donald.

"Twelve," I replied, "nearly thirteen." Two months shy of my birthday, to be exact.

"Won't drinking tea stunt your growth?" he asked rudely.

"Do I appear to be the least bit shrunken?" I responded, sitting up as tall as possible. Since I was half a head taller than most of the boys, nothing more needed to be said.

As soon as classes were over and everyone was filing out of the school, Arabella said, "Come with me to the Plaza. It's the center of town and everybody meets there after school."

Truthfully, I wasn't interested. I couldn't imagine anything worth seeing in this dull little village. I much preferred returning to Clem's house to check whether I'd had any mail from England.

"What about Este – I mean Steve? Won't he want to walk me home?" I asked. I had caught myself just in time. I much preferred the name Esteban, which was exotic like D'Artagnan from *The Three Musketeers*. But I had promised to call him Steve, at least in public.

"He's probably at the Plaza already, with his buddies," Arabella told me.

"Naturally," I said, not wanting her to know that I had been looking forward to the walk home with him.

The first thing I noticed at the Plaza was how sunshine dappled the leaves on the trees. Indeed there were real trees here, tall and green, and just starting to change color. On benches beneath the trees sat old men enjoying the warm afternoon light. The men courteously greeted everyone who passed, smiling and doffing their hats. And there were mothers pushing baby carriages. The women paused to chat with one another while their children ran after pigeons which flew along looking for the crumbs dropped by other children.

"What do you think of the Plaza?" said Arabella.

"It's lovely," I exclaimed. "Just like parks in London before the war."

We passed a handsome older gentleman in a light suit. *"Buenas dias, signoritas,"* he said.

We smiled courteously but a few steps later, I turned to Arabella. "Why does everyone here speak Spanish?"

"Not everyone does. It just seems like that." The dimples showed in her round cheeks. "But I can explain – look over there." She pointed to a long, low mud-colored building on one side of the Plaza that stretched the entire block. "That's the Palace of the Governors," Arabella said. "It's been there for three hundred years."

"A palace?" I exclaimed. "You can't mean you're calling that ugly building a palace? Why, it doesn't look anything like a palace!"

"No, I guess it doesn't look like Buckingham Palace," Arabella admitted.

"It certainly doesn't. Buckingham Palace is gorgeous," I said. "It has exquisite gardens and guards out front in smashing red uniforms."

"I've heard of those guards. They're very handsome, aren't they?" said Arabella. "Ooh, I can't wait to visit London! Have you ever been inside Buckingham Palace? Have you had tea with the Queen?"

"Of course I haven't had tea with the Queen," I snapped.

"I'm just an ordinary person. Nobody ordinary has tea with the Queen. You have to be a famous doctor or explorer."

"You don't seem ordinary to me," said Arabella. She seemed incapable of taking offense, no matter how snarly I sounded. "And the Queen is like the Mayor, isn't she? Well, that's the Mayor of Santa Fe over there."

She pointed to a nice-looking older gentleman with thick white hair who seemed happy to speak with anyone in the Plaza. Neither by his dress nor his manner could you possibly tell that he was the mayor of the town. "I'll introduce you to him, if you like," Arabella said.

"Another day, perhaps," I replied. "Does the mayor live in that old palace?" I pointed to the building on the side of the Plaza.

Arabella laughed. "No one lives there now. It's a museum. But a long time ago people lived there. When New Mexico was part of Spain. You see, all the land around here was part of Spain for hundreds of years."

"So that's why people here speak Spanish!"

Arabella nodded. "One day, the Indians got fed up with the Spanish. They weren't being treated very well. So they rebelled and killed a bunch of Spanish settlers. Everybody crowded into the Palace of the Governors. It wasn't a palace then, you see, it was a fort. The Spanish men, women and children squeezed in so they wouldn't be killed by the Indians."

"What a dreadful story." I looked around. "Where are the Indians now?"

"There they are." She pointed to a row of people sitting in front of the long, low mud-brown palace.

Oh, my goodness, I turned and stared. Real live Indians and

very nearby. I snatched my little red notebook from my pocket and began scribbling. Arabella eyed me with interest as I wrote:

It's only my second day in Santa Fe and already I am seeing Indians. They have very black hair and their skin is dark (not red). The Indians are seated on blankets. Some are also wrapped in colorfully striped blankets—blue, yellow, white. These Indians are not at all like the Indians you see at the cinema. The ones who wear war paint and ride ponies and shoot burning arrows at covered wagons. In fact, these Indians appear quiet and peaceful. I hope they remain so!

I put away my notebook, planning to make more notes about Indians in the future. Arabella was full of questions, however. "What's that little red book? What were you doing?"

"Oh, that was a gift from Father," I said. "He wants to know everything I see on my trip, so I'm recording it carefully."

Arabella's eyes grew large. "What a terrific idea. You must have a swell dad." It was impossible not to see the envy in her eyes.

"Oh, Father is wonderful," I said, thinking of his kind face. He would be so proud of me, too, taking notes like this. Plus, I supposed no one in my family had ever seen an American Indian; I was the first. "What are the Indians doing over there?"

"They come to town every day to sell the stuff they make," said Arabella. "Pottery and jewelry and rugs. Really keen stuff. Go and see for yourself."

I gazed again at the Indians, but didn't take a step in their direction.

"Don't worry," Arabella giggled. "No one will scalp you."

"Of course they won't," I said, but I wasn't ready to go any closer. Not today.

Meanwhile, Arabella drifted off to speak with friends on the Plaza. She seemed to know many people, even the mayor. She joked and laughed and flirted with young and old. How free and easy she behaved, as if everyone was a friend. It was my turn to feel envious.

I decided to sit down on a bench and wait for her. That's when my eyes fell upon a newspaper that had been left there. Picking it up, I saw a photo of a smoking bomber falling out of the sky. The headline read: *RAF BEATS OFF MASS AIR STRIKE.* Below were the words: *"British RAF fighters clashed with 300 German Warplanes in a terrific battle over the Thames…9 hours and 54 minutes of terror from the skies."*

Oh my God, my stomach hurt like it had been punched. How could I have forgotten? At this very moment on the other side of the world, bombs were dropping out of the sky. Men and women were running for their lives. Buildings were toppling over; smoke was rising; sirens were screaming and people were crying. The brave young men in the Royal Air Force were fighting back, fighting for the whole city. My city. I sank down on the bench, fighting back tears.

"What's wrong? Are you okay?" Arabella suddenly appeared at my side. "You look green – like you just saw La Llorona."

"La Llo-ron-a? Who – who's that?" I stammered, thrusting the newspaper behind me. I didn't want to tell Arabella why I had turned green. I didn't want to talk about it.

"She's the local ghost. A very scary lady," Arabella explained. "She haunts the river, crying for her drowned children."

"You don't mean the Santa Fe River? How could anyone drown in that little tiny stream?" I declared, glad to change the subject. I looked around. Everyone here was smiling. It was a beautiful afternoon. No one was thinking of the battles taking place on the other side of the ocean. Now I could see why some Americans didn't want their country to join England in the fight. How could you wish for the unhappiness of war to come to such a happy place?

Arabella laughed. "The river isn't always so teensy. Wait until the snows in the mountains melt in April, then you'll see how huge the river gets. Sometimes it floods."

I started to tell her that I wouldn't be here in the Spring. Ater all, if Mother was correct, I would be leaving in a few weeks, a few months at most. Then I thought of the newspaper photograph of the smoking RAF plane. What if the war lasted longer – for six or eight months or even for years? Oh no, I couldn't think that. It was too dreadful to imagine!

I turned quickly to Arabella. "What shall we do next? I'd like to see more of Santa Fe." Her brow furrowed a second, then she lit up. "I know what we can do. Follow me." We started across the street together but suddenly, she shouted, "Watch out!"

Looking down, I saw I had almost stepped in a big smelly pile of fresh animal droppings. Ugh.

"What's that?" I exclaimed, holding my nose.

"Just a little gift from the burros." Arabella's eyes were mischievous.

"The what?" I said.

"Come on, I'll show you." She led me down the street, past a row of stores, one right after another. Most of the shops carried ordinary things - shoes, clothes, books, pots and pans, dishes, toys – just what you'd see in any small town. But a few shop windows had quite remarkable displays – one was filled with shiny silver and turquoise jewelry. Another contained fancy leather saddles, little Indian dolls – nothing I had ever seen before.

Arabella paused for a moment, too. "That's mostly for tourists," said Arabella. "A lot of people visit Santa Fe from around the world."

I gazed with interest, wishing we could go inside. After all, I was a sort of tourist here, a visitor. But Arabella didn't tarry; she was already halfway down the street. I had to run to catch up with her. A moment later, however, we both halted again. Plastered to the wall, smack before our eyes was a giant poster. In it, the gorgeous English actress, Vivian Leigh, swooned in the arms of the incredibly handsome Clark Gable. The muscles in his arms were immense as he gripped her waist.

"*Gone With the Wind*," Arabella murmured reverently. "I've seen it eight times. How 'bout you?"

"I haven't yet seen it, but I'm dying to go," I replied. "Everyone says Vivian Leigh has completely smothered her English accent. She sounds exactly like a Southern belle from Georgia."

The marquee above said Lensic Theater. I wondered if that was where Esteban had seen newsreels of British bombers. But it was hard to imagine a boy like him sitting through a romance like *Gone With the Wind* even once.

"We have lots of movie theaters," said Arabella as if guessing my thought. "People in Santa Fe love the movies!" Then she headed around a corner. I rushed after her, turning into a small alleyway where a row of shaggy little beasts stood patiently.

"These are burros," exclaimed Arabella. "Aren't they sweet?" The docile animals with big, gentle sloping eyes were munching hay. Each carried a giant load of sticks, almost as large as the burros.

"Do they bite?" I asked, stepping closer.

"Sometimes," said Arabella, stroking one. "But not often." I reached over and touched its thick fur. It felt like an untidy wool blanket. What a dear creature! I considered taking out my notebook again and writing something about burros. But just then, Arabella piped up. "Aren't you starving?"

"Of course," I said. "I'm absolutely famished. Isn't it nearly teatime?"

"Teatime?" Arabella giggled. "You are so adorable. There's no teatime here. We'll go to Zook's Pharmacy and get a shake."

"Go where? Get what? What did you say?"

"A milkshake," shouted Arabella. She was already hurrying back up the street toward the Plaza. A few moments later, we stood on the corner across the street from the pharmacy. To my surprise, Esteban and three or four of his friends were leaning against the building. They were wearing the same blue dungarees as earlier in the day. But now their plaid cotton shirts weren't tucked in and they didn't look like students. Somehow, they looked older and tougher.

I smiled and waved, but Esteban turned his head as if he didn't see me. He was gripping some sort of wooden box in one hand. A bit hurt, I asked, "Why isn't Esteban—I mean Steve—more friendly?"

Arabella shrugged. "He may be embarrassed for you to see him at work."

"At work? Is he working?" I turned to look at him again.

"After school, he often shines shoes on the Plaza," Arabella explained. "Lots of boys do it to earn extra cash."

"Esteban is a shoeshine boy?" My eyes widened with amazement. Shoeshine boys in London were ragged, often dirty youngsters. They carried boxes filled with brown and black wax and brushes and rags as they dashed from one person to another in search of a few pence. Shoeshine boys were among the poorest, roughest people in the city. Not at all the kind of person that I would ever know or speak to.

"His father is dead," said Arabella. "Dolores works hard, but she has a big family. Steve has four younger brothers and sisters to care for."

"I see," I said, still a bit dumbfounded. Shining shoes was a perfectly reasonable job, of course. But the idea that I *personally* knew a shoeshine boy – someone I talked to and walked to school with – was simply extraordinary.

"You do want a milkshake, don't you?" said Arabella. "Zook's has got the most super-duper shakes in town."

"Of course I do," I said, starting to cross the street with Arabella a step behind. As I drew closer, Esteban's face turned a shade rosier. I considered whether or not to speak to him.

"Hello, Steve," I said. "Nice to see you." My voice sounded a little squeaky.

He glanced up, his lips in a tight line. "Hey," he mumbled, then glanced away again.

I smiled, brightly as possible, and walked into the pharmacy with Arabella close behind. The two of us chose stools at the counter and studied the menu. Oh, my goodness, what scrumptious selections – chocolate drift, banana split, hot fudge sundae. How would I ever choose among these delightful concoctions? For a moment I almost wished I could remain in Santa Fe long enough to sample them all.

A tall woman with thick braids on her head and a little dog on a leash walked past. "Hello, Miss Zook," said Arabella politely. The woman looked down at her sharply and nodded. "Good day, Arabella."

Then a waitress with short frizzy hair and a pencil stuck behind one ear, demanded, "What you gals gonna have?"

I dumped all the change from my pocket onto the counter. On the last day of our voyage, Captain Wingate gave me American money in exchange for my English pound notes. I had used some money on the train with Hamilton. But the pennies, nickels, dimes and quarters still confused me. Pushing the pile of coins toward the waitress, I asked, "Do I have enough for a milkshake?"

The girl looked amused. "You have enough for six milkshakes." She took a few coins and pushed the remainder in my direction. I chose a chocolate flavor shake and Arabella picked an orange fizz, which matched her hair.

"I'm so glad you've come to Santa Fe and we can be friends," she said, her freckled face glowing.

I smiled back. Yes, indeed, it was extremely nice to have a friend, my first American friend.

Chapter 8

26 September 1940
Dear Willy,
   I have to tell the truth. My first
impressions of New Mexico were pretty
ghastly. Dry, rocky land, almost no
trees, starving sheep, mud-colored
houses, dirt streets and a trickle of
water they call a river. Also, almost
no one here speaks English correctly.
People say the oddest things, then they
claim I talk strangely. Lots of people
don't speak English at all - they speak
Spanish, making me feel as if I was
standing on a street in Madrid. Despite
the difficulties, I am trying very hard
to be a good sport. As Father said, I am

*encountering many new things. And
I try my best to enjoy them. Today I
patted a sweet furry little donkey that
they call a burro. Also I made a new
friend named Arabella and I drank a
delicious thick ice creamy drink called
a chocolate milkshake.*

I put down my pen, picturing Willy sipping a shake. He certainly would enjoy that. I wondered what he was doing that very minute? I was still a bit confused about the difference in the times between Santa Fe and London. When was it morning, afternoon or night over there? Was it still yesterday or already tomorrow?

Wherever Willy was at that instant, I hoped that he was safe and that Mother and Father and Alfie were safe, too. Thinking of them made me ache all over as if I had a fever. I supposed that's why the feeling is called home-sickness.

"Hey, gal," Clem called out cheerfully as she entered the house. "How was your day?"

"Very well, thank you," I replied. "Here's today's post. I fetched it from the box. I hope you don't mind."

"Thanks, Bea," said Clem, taking the envelopes and glancing at them. She tore one open and read the letter inside.

"Drat," she exclaimed.

"Is anything wrong?" I asked.

Clem shrugged. "Just the usual problem—too many poor people and not enough to go around. Not enough food, medicine, you name it. And we're not likely to get any more supplies 'til next year. Maybe not then, either."

"I don't understand," I said.

She considered how to explain. "Well, Bea, I bet you've always had plenty of oatmeal in your bowl for breakfast each morning."

"Of course there was enough," I said. "And we used to have platters of bacon and eggs and toast and marmalade and other good things, too. The war has made it much harder to get butter and eggs and meat. But we still had plenty to eat."

"Then you may be surprised to learn that not every child has such a wonderful breakfast," she responded.

"I'm sure there are a few who have only oatmeal," I replied.

"Honestly, Bea, I've seen lots of children," Clem said, "who'd be happy to have anything for breakfast. Anything at all."

Her words made me think of Alphonse, Alfred and Andre who were so very hungry they wanted to eat everything in sight. I thought also of Esteban working for extra money to feed his family. He might only earn a few nickels and dimes in an afternoon. Still, he worked every day just for that.

When I glanced up, Clem was gazing at me thoughtfully. "My Mom and Dad always told us kids to count our blessings. Especially when there was enough on the table to feed all of us, even if it was simple." She grinned. "Now let's see what Dolores has fixed us for tonight."

Again we dined on a big stew of beans, meat, and cheese with tortillas. Just as before, as soon as she'd polished her plate, Clem began asking questions. She was the most curious-about-things person I had ever met. Tonight I found it much easier to talk and to tell her everything that had happened that day.

"So Arabella showed you around town," Clem mused. "She's a good guide, I bet. Though kind of a scatter-brain."

"What do you mean?" I asked.

"Arabella doesn't use the good sense she was born with," said Clem. "There's nothing stupid about her. She just doesn't always bother to think." She pointed her fork at me for emphasis. "That's a mistake no woman worth her salt can make."

I sat for a moment, pondering what she had said. The truth was that I had never been encouraged to believe thinking was an activity intended for girls. Mother emphasized looks and charm above all else. In fact, when Great-Aunt Augusta suggested young women ought to have "something going on upstairs," Mother had responded, "Oh yes, some girls are smart but you mustn't get a reputation for being brainy. Men don't care for brainy girls."

I was sincerely glad that Clem didn't agree with Mother. I had always liked being able to think things through clearly. Besides, now I was putting myself in the role of an explorer like Mary Kingsley. Quick thinking had saved Miss Kingsley many times.

We were still chatting when the telephone rang loudly. Clem immediately went to the hall and picked up the receiver. I heard her say, "Yep...Nope...Don't worry, I'll be there in a jiffy!" Putting down the phone, Clem rushed to grab a jacket. Her face was serious. "I'm heading over to the Indian Hospital. Somebody's brought in a boy in bad shape." She grabbed her satchel and started toward the door.

I had already begun clearing the table on my own when a thought darted into my mind. "Excuse me, Clem," I called out. "May I come along?"

She paused, surprised. "Don't you have homework?"

"Just a little. And I would really like to go with you. I want to see what nurses do."

Clem considered a brief moment. "Okay, gal, but hurry!"

I ran and grabbed a thick, green wool sweater. The night air in Santa Fe, I'd discovered, was very chilly. Minutes later, the two of us were buzzing through the quiet town in Maude, the truck. We reached the Indian Hospital at the edge of town. A long, low building, it was a bit grander than I had expected. I grew more and more curious as we walked up to the door. What would it be like inside?

A girl opened the door for us. Though she appeared older than me, she was several inches shorter. Her round dark face was framed by a row of black bangs across her forehead. The remainder of her shiny black hair was pulled back in one long braid that reached far down her back. She seemed both extremely calm and alert.

"Hello, Ana," said Clem. "I'm glad you phoned. This is Beatrice."

Ana turned her smiling eyes in my direction. "Ana's a student at the Indian school who helps out in the hospital," Clem explained. "They only have one doctor, Dr. Johnson, and one nurse. They call me when they need help."

Inside, the Indian Hospital was very plain and simple. Two years before, I had gone to a London hospital when Great-Aunt Augusta was ill with pneumonia. The huge stone and brick building had long corridors and countless doors. Nurses in starched white uniforms hurried past. The rules for visitors and family members were strict. Only one person could enter the sickroom at a time. Nothing in that London Hospital resembled anything I saw here.

Ana led us past wooden benches where patients sat for visits with the doctor. The benches were empty now. We followed her down a short corridor to a large room with 14 beds in two rows. The place was warm, almost hot, and smelled sharply of antiseptic. The beds were neatly made; most were empty. Next to one, I saw a couple standing, stiff with worry.

The father was tall, with broad shoulders and arms that seemed sturdy enough to pull up a stump or push a boulder out of the way. His eyes were sunk deep in his face; his mouth was a straight line with deep creases on either side. His long black hair was pulled back into a knot at the back of his head and tied with a bit of reddish string. The mother was very thin. She wore a black shawl over her head so I could barely see her face. She was leaning over the bed and her strong fingers grasped her son's hand.

The little boy, age 7 or 8, rolled back and forth deliriously on the bed. Though open and staring, his eyes seemed not to see us. His thin cotton shirt and pants were damp with sweat and clung to his thin body. The sheet beneath him also seemed soiled and grimy.

Clem asked the parents a few questions. Then she shook her head and went to look for something, muttering, "I'll see how much anti-tetanus serum is left." She returned shortly with a hypodermic needle, light glinting on the thin metal. The boy was still thrashing around. His father and mother could barely manage to hold on to him. He seemed stronger than an ordinary child, pulling and twisting against their grip like a wild animal. His jaw was tightly shut and his lips pulled back against his teeth in a strange smile.

"Hold him still," Clem commanded. His parents grasped

him firmly. I shrank back in the corner, glad to be out of the way. Clem seized the boy's arm tightly – I could see why she kept her nails trimmed short – and carefully stuck in the needle, which remained in his arm as she slowly injected the serum. I held my breath – if the boy suddenly jerked, the needle might break. But he didn't stir. For a few moments, he lay limp against the mattress, looking weak and fragile as a paper cutout.

When the injection was finished, Clem turned to the parents. Her face was somber. "You got here just in time. Did you come far?"

The man, speaking tersely, answered, "Taos."

"Well, you're welcome to sleep here tonight," she said. "We've done the best we could. I'll go by St. Vincent's Hospital in town and fetch more serum. Then I can give him another injection in the morning."

The father nodded. The mother murmured something in a strange language and pressed Clem's hand. I hoped we could finally leave, but Clem wasn't ready to go. "Let's try to change this bed," she murmured.

Ana quickly left and returned with an armful of fresh linen. Clem glanced in my direction. "Want to lend us a hand, Bea?"

"M-me?" I stammered. How could I touch those sticky, smelly sheets?

"Never mind." Clem turned to Ana and the two deftly began changing the sheets. They were so quick and skillful at removing the dirty sheets, they barely disturbed the sick boy. Then they spread clean white sheets beneath him.

I stood watching, hands at my side, feeling rather dumb and useless.

Finally Clem fluffed the pillow under the boy's head and spoke quietly to the boy's parents. Then Ana led us back out to the entrance.

A minute later, we stood outside. Gratefully, I sucked in the cold night air. The hospital room had been tense and a little scary. Plus, I wished that I had helped, even a little. On the drive home, Clem remained silent for a few minutes. Finally, she said, "The worst feeling in the world is when you can't save a kid's life 'cause you don't have what you need."

"Does that often happen?" I asked.

"Sometimes we run short of tetanus serum. It will get even worse now that all the money and supplies are going to the Defense Department, just in case we get in the war."

The war? Clem must mean the war in Europe. My head started buzzing. Would the United States enter the war soon? I remembered the people on the train. If the United States did enter the war, would it come to the aid of Britain? Surely the answer was yes. But I didn't absolutely know for certain. Not after hearing the comments of those people on the train and the boy, Donald, in my class. People in this country didn't all think the same way about anything.

When we reached Clem's house, she turned to me and said, "I'm glad you came tonight. You probably got a heckuva'lot more learning than reading a school textbook."

I nodded. "It's hard work being a nurse, isn't it?"

Clem smiled wearily. "Hard work, but good work."

Climbing into bed that night, I was more tired than usual. I hadn't done anything, but I had seen a great deal. I had seen stuff I could never have imagined in my fine London home. And next time, I swore to myself, I would behave better, I'd try to help, I would...

As my eyes were closing, I again thought of the war. I said a little prayer to people in the United States. "Please, help my country, please, please, please."

Chapter Nine

The next day after school, Arabella suggested we go meet her uncle who lived next door to Clem. "He's a real sweetheart and a rather famous painter," she said, imitating my accent in a comical way.

The two of us walked over to a large mud-colored house with a high wall around it. Arabella motioned to me, mischievously, as she opened a little white gate.

"Uncle Diego doesn't like me to visit while he's working," Arabella whispered, "but we can peek in the window."

Peek in the window? I paused. What would Great-Aunt Augusta say about that? But the unstoppable Arabella had already disappeared around the corner of the house. I decided to follow and found her standing in front of a little window. She put a finger to her lips, motioning for me to be silent. Then she carefully opened the blue-painted wood shutters and peered in. "See, there he is!" Arabella whispered, pointing inside.

Looking into a large open room, I immediately spied her Uncle Diego. He was a tall, serious-looking man with thin black hair plastered across a high pale forehead. He was dressed in a dark coat, light shirt and tie, like he was going to church, not painting a picture. One hand tightly grasped a large paintbrush and he studied the canvas on an easel before him like it was a prayer book.

"Oh, my gosh! Look what he's painting," Arabella gasped, her eyes wide with astonishment.

I shifted my gaze to the other end of the room. Very clearly in view was a tall woman with thick, glossy black hair piled on top of her head. She was lounging the length of a couch with a yellow and blue striped blanket casually draped over her torso. But from her pearly white shoulders and bare thighs, it appeared the lady must be completely naked beneath the blanket.

"Goodness gracious!" I gasped out loud. Uncle Diego must have heard because he whirled around so fast that a great glob of paint flew off his brush into the air.

"Who is it? Who's there?" he shouted, and ran toward the door. Arabella tried to escape, but I was glued to the spot. Uncle Diego rushed out the door and came toward me, yelling, "Who are you? Who the heck are you?" Waving that paintbrush like a sword, he was a frightening sight.

I couldn't straight away open my mouth and when at last I did, no sound came out. Uncle Diego was so upset I thought he might strike me with the paintbrush. Fortunately, Arabella returned, grinning sheepishly.

"Oh, Uncle, I'm sorry." Then she started to giggle. I'm not at all sure what, at that moment, was so funny. Maybe it was just sheer relief from being scared, but I, too, started to giggle. Soon the two of us nearly collapsed to the ground, we were laughing so hard.

Uncle Diego ignored our silliness, but he lost his grim expression. "Arabella, I've told you again and again not to interrupt my work!"

"I promise, I promise, I won't do it again." Arabella sounded contrite, but she winked at me.

Uncle Diego looked fondly at his niece. I guessed she could do much worse things and still be forgiven. He gestured toward the studio. "Come on in, you rascals."

The large, high-ceilinged room was extremely messy and cluttered with every possible item. Stacks of frames and canvases leaned against the walls; bottles, jars, coffee cans and tubes of paint covered shelves and tables. Scattered all around was an odd array of dried flowers, bones, rocks and shells.

I was almost afraid to look in the direction of his model. But when I finally dared, the woman seated on the couch was wearing a thin pink and blue kimono. I daresay she was still quite naked underneath. But if so, she didn't appear in the least bit concerned.

"Why, you gals certainly are the mischievous ones, aren't you?" The woman had a drawl that reminded me of Hamilton, the train porter, but much more pronounced. Every word, even very short ones, was drawn out into two or three syllables.

"Where did you come from?" Arabella asked bluntly.

"Excuse me, Arabella," said Uncle Diego, "I don't think I've introduced my friend Lola."

"I come from Alabama, originally," replied Lola. In her mouth, the words stretched out like a piece of taffy. She stressed the word "originally" as if she'd been to many other places, as well.

"So how did you get here?" Arabella didn't seem pleased to meet her uncle's new friend.

"We-e-ll," said Lola, leaning back on the couch, looking pleased that she'd been asked, "I was traveling to California, to Hollywood in fact, on the Southwest Chief when the train stopped in Albuquerque. You know the trip to Albuquerque is very long and very tee-dee-us, so I just stepped off the train for a few minutes to give myself a little breather." She stretched her long arms to show us what that was like. The kimono fell open and nearly revealed her very white ample bosom. Arabella and I stared shamelessly, mesmerized by the sight.

"On the train platform were these Indians, the nicest folks, selling stuff. Baskets, rugs, jewelry, you know what I mean. It was all just so fascinating to me, I took my time looking. Finally, I went to the ladies room in the station for half a minute to powder my nose." She paused and turned her head in profile so we could clearly see her sharp turned-up nose – the one she had needed to powder.

"And then what happened?" Arabella demanded.

"Why, dar-lin, I simply missed hearing the train whistle. By the time I reached the platform, the train was halfway to Gallup, with no intention of coming back."

Arabella whirled around to face her uncle. "So how did you meet Lola?" The tables had turned. Now the tall, serious man looked sheepish.

"I happened to be in Albuquerque buying paints. I saw this lovely lady obviously needing help. And I'm always looking for good models," he finished lamely. Arabella shook her head like this was an old story.

"I'm a superior model. I've been told that many times before," said Lola.

Eager to change the subject, Uncle Diego turned to me. "So who are you?"

"Can't you guess, Uncle? She's the English girl staying with Clem," announced Arabella. "But don't offer her tea and crumpets! She prefers American milkshakes!"

Uncle Diego looked at me with sharp interest, as if he planned to paint my portrait next. "I would have thought English girls knew better than snooping around people's yards," he said.

"Of course we do," I replied huffily.

"My niece probably sets a bad example," said Uncle Diego, but now he seemed more relaxed. "So where is Clem today?"

"I'm not sure. I believe she's gone to an Indian village," I replied

"An Indian pueblo, you mean." He looked at me. "You know what that is?"

I shook my head. I hadn't the foggiest idea.

"Lots of Indians in little mud houses," exclaimed Arabella.

"Arabella," said Uncle Diego sternly, "I don't like the way you make that sound. You know most people in Santa Fe live in mud houses, too." He gestured around his spacious studio. "Like this one. It's built of hard mud bricks called adobe and it is every bit as good as any building in the world. If not better."

I looked around. Mud? The walls were painted white with high-beamed ceilings. It certainly didn't look like mud! Was Clem's house also mud? Did that mean I was living in a mud house?

"I'm an Indian," Lola broke in. We all turned to stare at her. "Pure Cherokee blood runs through my veins." Her skin was chalk white and her eyes were violet. "On my great-grandmother's side, three times removed." We must have all looked doubtful because she touched her fingers to her face. "See these high cheek-bones? That's how you can tell."

Lola looked as much like an Indian as Cook's sister, Miss Frimby, who came from Scotland. By now, however, Uncle Diego seemed ready to end the visit. "You girls are taking up my precious painting time. I bet you can find something else to do."

"Young girls usually can," drawled Lola, reclining back upon the couch and lighting a cigarette in a long cigarette holder. I was still hypnotized by the sight of her, but Arabella signaled to me. "C'mon, Beatrice. We get the point."

She led the way out of the studio and back to Clem's house, imitating Lola in the most hilarious way. "Oh, Diego, you remind me of my dahling Rhett Butler…"

I giggled. "Does Lola sound like Scarlett O'Hara in *Gone With the Wind*?"

Arabella nodded. "She sure does. My uncle is a wonderful painter, but he's an idiot when it comes to romance."

"Really?" I wanted to know more.

Arabella sighed dramatically. "He believes every pretty lady is a muse who inspires his art. More often she's an artsy woman who bamboozles him."

"Do you think your uncle is in love with Lola?" I asked. Any form of love seemed very strange and mysterious to me.

"Well, I wouldn't call it serious love, more like puppy love."

"Your uncle is rather a big puppy," I replied.

"Raw-tha a big puppy," Arabella imitated my accent. And it sounded truly hilarious the way she said it. We both started laughing again and we laughed all the way back to Clem's house.

Chapter Ten

A week later at school, we'd barely sat down at our desks when a skinny, freckled boy named Harry ran in the room shouting, "A bear! There's a bear outside!" Every student hopped up from their desk and ran out the door, not even bothering to grab a coat or a hat. I was the last outside and minutes later, I too stood shivering in the schoolyard. All the students were gazing up into a tall evergreen tree. A cold wind was blowing and little snowflakes were drifting down from the grey sky. The white icy flakes tickled my nose. Arabella dashed by, looking enchanted. "What a surprise. Snow in October!"

"Look, see, there he is!" Harry yelled, pointing up. I squinted and could only manage to make out a large, brown blob among the branches.

Arabella shouted at the boy, "You don't know if it's a he or she, do you?"

Esteban said, "The bears ain't getting enough to eat in the forest, that's why they come into town." He imitated pulling back the string of a bow and taking aim. "Good bear skin," he muttered. "Make a great blanket or rug."

Donald Riggsbee sauntered over and stood near me. "My father doesn't like President Roosevelt. He wants Wendell Willkie to win. Dad belongs to the America First Committee. That's a group of Americans who don't want us to fight another stupid war. They're real good Americans, too, like Charles Lindbergh, the first man to fly across the Atlantic Ocean. And Walt Disney—you know who he is?"

"What do you mean, "a stupid war"?" I demanded.

"It's just a big squabble between the countries in Europe. That's what Dad says. He works on the newspaper, so he knows all the news. He says those countries over there never get along," said Donald. "We'd be fools to get a lot of Americans killed again like in the last big war. That was called "The War to End All Wars," but that sure didn't happen, did it?" His mouth contorted in an ugly sneer.

"Far too many Englishmen were killed in that war, too." I explained, trying to remain calm. "But still, we can't give up now, can we? And we need help from your country." But Donald wasn't even listening any more. He walked away to bother someone else. What a creep, I thought, using a new word I learned from

Arabella. What did he know about anything? He was just repeating what his father said.

Mrs. Montoya began ushering us all back inside. Passing by Donald, I reached to the ground, scraped up a little snowball and hurled it right at him. The ball smacked him right on the ear. Whirling around furiously, Donald threw a snowball back at me. I ducked and it hit another girl. Soon, to the dismay of Mrs. Montoya, all the students were pelting one another with snowballs. Poor Donald Riggsbee got *clobbered*—another useful word I learned from Arabella.

Hearing new words and writing them down in my notebook was a fun game I had invented. I always put in a sentence for each word, showing how it was used.

> doggone – "That doggone coyote has been fussing at the chickens again."
> gussy up – "That lady in the big hat sure did gussy up to come downtown."
> doozie – "Hey, what a doozie of a pitch Esteban just threw."
> gunk – "Phew! Did you see all the gunk that boy put in his hair?"

I heard many of the words from Clem. "That's 'cause I come from Oklahoma," she told me. "There's a lot of colorful language comes from Oklahoma." But I also gathered words from Arabella. She enjoyed knowing the latest slang like "creep" for boys like Donald and "bebop" for the lively music she listened to on the radio.

I felt like an explorer learning new languages. Mary Kingsley,

I knew, had mastered several during her African travels. But the true reason I kept this list was to tell Father when I returned home. He'd laugh and laugh to hear words like "doozie" or "gunk". And I so longed to hear his laugh as in the old days before the war.

That evening, after dinner, Clem and I cleaned up together. Putting away the dishes, I said, "Donald Riggsbee says Wendell Willkie may beat Mr. Roosevelt in the election for president. What do you think, Clem?"

"Gosh, Bea, no one can say for sure," she said. "Elections are like horse races. You can't ever tell who's gonna win 'til the first horse crosses the finish line."

Oh dear, I hated for Clem to sound so uncertain. Everyone knew that President Roosevelt and the British Prime Minister Winston Churchill were great chums. I had seen a picture in the newspaper of the two smoking cigars together. According to the news on the radio, Roosevelt was already sending ships with supplies from the United States to England.

"It's true Mr. Willkie has many supporters in New Mexico," said Clem. "Especially in the south of the state where there are a lot of ranches."

"But I don't understand," I said. "I thought everyone liked President Roosevelt."

"Many people do like him. Poor people specially love him 'cause he's helped them a lot," said Clem. "But wealthy Americans aren't so fond of FDR. They say he's betrayed their class. Also, he's running for a third term. There's never been an American president in office for a third term. Some people don't like that."

"But if Mr. Willkie wins, will the United States help Britain?"

Clem shrugged. "I don't know, Bea. Mr. Willkie says he supports England, if it doesn't mean going to war. He and the Republican Party don't want our country in this fight."

My heart sank. The election was only a month away. What if Wendell Willkie won and America didn't join the fight? What would happen to Britain if it had to battle alone against Germany? I remembered what Father had said. Could England truly lose the war? And if it did, what would happen to me? Would I ever be able to return home?

Fortunately, my unhappy thoughts were interrupted by a dreadful racket in the backyard. Dolores kept several guinea hens out there with the chickens, and they were loudly squawking.

"Now what's that ruckus about?" said Clem.

"Maybe it's a bear!" I exclaimed.

Clem had another idea. She grabbed the broom and ran outside, swinging it over her head. "Darn coyote, going after our chicks again."

We raced out into the night, but just missed seeing whatever caused the commotion. The creature left a big hole in the wire of the henhouse fence. Clem got out some tools and mended the break as skillfully as if she was suturing a wound. I watched her work, though. I was jumping up and down to stay warm. It was lovely to be outside in the starlit darkness. "What a gorgeous night!" I exclaimed. "Don't you think so, Clem?"

In London, clouds often covered the night sky. Or the air was filled with smoke from coal-burning fires. Here in New Mexico, the night sky was clear and immense like a vast, black scarf glittering with sequins.

"You're right, Bea. The night sky is a real show-stopper," said

Clem.

Despite the cold, we stood outside another ten minutes while she pointed out constellations. "You probably know the Big Dipper and the North Star," she said. "But have you ever seen the Milky Way?"

I gazed up at a glowing mantle of light high above. What a stupendous sight! I sucked in icy air scented pungently from the piñon logs that burned in nearly every fireplace.

"My Dad knew the name of just about every star," Clem said, still gazing up.

"Every star?" I was amazed.

"Almost. He was a teacher, but it wasn't book-learning he knew best," said Clem. "His world was the out-of-doors. He never tired of telling us kids about birds and trees and rocks and butterflies."

"Your father was a school teacher?" I asked.

"Yep, he taught at an Indian day school in Oakley, Oklahoma," she replied. "It was a boy's school but my little sisters and I went there 'cause there was no other school for miles around."

"You went to school with Indians?" I had met Ana at the Indian Hospital and seen the row of Indians under the Palace portal. Still, I imagined Indian children with feathers stuck in their dark hair and tomahawks under their desks.

"I sure did," said Clem. "Cherokee, Chickasaw, Creek, Ponca, Muscogee and others. There's a heap of Indians in Oklahoma."

"Those are the names of Indians?"

"They're different Indian tribes. See, Oklahoma got all the Indians that were forced to leave other places in the United States. People in the South and the East weren't so hospitable to the

Indians living there," explained Clem. "So they pushed them all into Oklahoma."

"My goodness, Clem, you certainly know a lot," I said.

"I know a lot about this country." She grinned. "But I bet you know more about the people in England – the Saxons, the Celts, the Vikings and Normans. I never could get them all straight."

"English history is a bit complicated," I admitted. "But please tell me, what was it like going to school with Indian children?"

"Just the same as going to school with anybody. Those Indian kids were no different – they'd laugh when something was funny and cry when something was sad." She shook her head. "But, golly, those little Indian boys sure loved to play tricks on me and my sisters."

"What sort of tricks?"

"Putting frogs or snakes in our lunch pails, that kind of thing."

"Snakes! How awful!" I said. "Weren't you scared?"

"It does make you jump to see a little green snake crawl out of your lunch pail, when you reach for a ham sandwich," said Clem.

Her words made me laugh. Finally, shivering with cold, we went back inside and each had a cup of hot cocoa before going to bed.

It wasn't nearly as funny when I saw my first horrid creature.

One evening, I was getting ready for a nice hot bath as usual. I turned on the steamy hot water, then undressed. As I sat idly daydreaming, water flooded into the big old tub. All of a sudden, I glanced at the edge of the tub and spied the most disgusting thing.

"Auuugh!" I screamed. The creature was long and narrow and appeared to have hundreds of legs, which scrambled around the slippery tub. I screamed again and again. "Help! Someone please help me!" Then I ran out in the hall with a big white bath towel wrapped round me. Thank goodness, within seconds, Dolores arrived. She grabbed a piece of bathroom tissue, then plucked up the squiggly monster and flushed it down the toilet. I carefully entered the bathroom again, looking in every corner to see if the creature had any sisters or brothers.

"Please stay here with me," I pleaded. "Just in case." So Dolores sat with me until the tub was filled and we were absolutely certain no other little monster might appear.

I told Clem as soon as she came home, assuming she would be as upset as I had been. But she didn't seem to think I had experienced a major calamity. Calmly taking off her coat and putting away her gloves and scarf, she said, "You saw a centipede. They're pretty common around here."

I gasped, "You mean I might see another?"

Clem nodded. "Most likely."

"From now on," I demanded, "Dolores must inspect the bathroom before I go in."

Clem looked at me a moment. "No, Bea, that won't be necessary. Dolores is much too busy to be your personal servant. You saw how she got rid of the bug, didn't you?"

I nodded.

"Well, next time you can do the same."

"I couldn't possibly. I hate insects."

Clem smiled. "You hate all insects? There's quite a variety, you know, from ladybugs to hornets, from gnats to dragonflies."

"I don't like little crawly things that might climb on me." I shuddered.

"Only ten-year-old boys like little crawly things, Bea," said Clem. "But there's a few things in life you gotta get used to or you won't amount to much. And a bug or two in the bathtub is one of 'em."

I opened my mouth to protest but her mouth was set firmly in a straight line. So I knew the matter was closed.

12 October 1940
Dear Willy,

Please look up the word "centipede" in Father's encyclopedia. There you will see a picture of an insect with dozens of little legs. It is truly gruesome. There was one in my bathtub tonight. They can sting, which I'm sure hurts quite badly. That's why I am extremely glad that I didn't faint as Mother surely would have done. If I had fainted, the centipede might have crawled all over me, which is the most horrid thing I can imagine! Clem says not to worry, most insects are completely harmless. But she says one must look out for scorpions and black widow spiders. The poison from a black widow can kill you with one bite. So I always watch where I put my fingers. Still, I know that the dangers of the Wild West are much less terrible than the dangers you face each day. You needn't worry. I'm doing A-okay, as they say here in the States.

Much love,

Beatrice

Indeed, I was A-okay. Though not very brave. Centipedes, after all, were not nearly as dangerous as crocodiles. Mary Kingsley had once encountered an eight-foot crocodile while paddling her dug-out canoe alone through a swamp. The giant monster crawled onto the front of her canoe and tried to overturn it. She smacked it on the head with her paddle and the beast swam away.

How did explorers like Miss Kingsley become so brave? Could I ever become brave like that? Pondering this question, I fell asleep in my snug bed.

Chapter Eleven

A few days after the centipede invaded my bath, Arabella announced that she was leaving school early that day.

"I'm experiencing a very low point in my life," she declared, laying a hand on her forehead.

"What's wrong?" I asked.

"I'm worried about Uncle Diego."

I knew that Uncle Diego acted like a father to Arabella. She had told me that her mother was an opera singer, a beautiful, remarkable woman who didn't stay attached to any man for very long. "And that includes my father," said Arabella, "who was also a singer." In fact, that was all she knew about her father, that he was a superb tenor.

While her mother was out of town, Uncle Diego looked after his niece. And she looked after him as well.

"Is Uncle Diego still in love with Lola?"

Arabella shook her head. "It's very sad. A few days ago, Lola caught the train to California. This time, I guess, she heard the whistle blow."

"Is he so very unhappy?" I asked, trying not to smile.

"I think it's the worst love affair he's had yet," said Arabella. "He's so miserable that he's quit painting. I have to go over there and cheer him up."

"What will you do?" I inquired.

"We'll mope and eat." She smiled. "That means that he mopes and I eat. After a while, we both feel a whole lot better."

Arabella wrote an excuse for herself with an elegant unreadable signature that she claimed was her mother's. She gave the note to the principal, who merely glanced at it and let her go. Everyone seemed accustomed to Arabella's way of doing things. And no one wished to stand in her way.

So that afternoon I ended up walking home from school by myself. I knew the way, of course. Actually there were several routes, long and short, direct and meandering. I chose my favorite, walking along the Santa Fe River. By now I was used to the fact that it wasn't a real river. In fact I had grown rather fond of the sweet little stream. It gurgled along happily beneath huge cottonwood trees now covered with golden leaves. Through the shimmering leaves, I glimpsed the bright blue sky. It was a lovely day and unlike the intense blazing sunlight of a month ago, the sun was now gentle and friendly.

As I walked along the river, dozens of crisp cottonwood leaves crunched beneath my feet. I stooped down and found one that looked like a little yellow fan. What a magical shape! I picked up another, waved it in the air, then let it loose to fly freely. The leaf twirled round and round until it landed in the water. I watched the current pull each spinning leaf downstream.

Suddenly I felt someone's eyes on me. Glancing up, I found Esteban standing on the other side of the stream, not far away. Had he been watching me for long? Why wasn't he working on the Plaza? Arabella had told me that there were fewer tourists downtown as the days grew shorter and colder. Perhaps there wasn't much business for shoeshine boys.

Esteban and I still walked to school together each morning. We talked about what the British bomber planes were doing to defend my country. He was still impressed by Britain's pluck and determination. "If the U.S. gets in the war, I'll sign up right away," he said boldly.

I was partly pleased by the image of him fighting with the Brits. Then I thought of how Dolores would feel about her oldest son joining up. She would feel as badly as Mother would about Willy. Maybe worse, because Dolores depended on his help.

But the war was not Esteban's main topic of conversation during our daily walks. It was baseball, the game played by every boy in the schoolyard before and after school. His favorite team was called the Dodgers. He explained to me that the Dodgers played baseball in Brooklyn, which was a part of New York City. Esteban's biggest dream was to go to New York and watch the Dodgers play. "You can go, too," he told me. "We'll go in the summer and eat hot dogs and big dill pickles."

"Hot dogs? Pickles?" I remembered the delicious hot dogs I'd eaten on the train. But I knew Esteban had no idea how far away Brooklyn was. He had only once been as far as Albuquerque. He certainly didn't know what it was like to travel for days and days on a train.

"I'd love to go to a Dodgers game with you next summer," I said. It was a safe promise since I was confident that I wouldn't be here then.

That afternoon, walking along the river, however, I was not in a mood to even chat with Esteban. In fact I had a good reason to be unhappy with him. Walking swiftly, I tried to lose him, but he quickly caught up.

For a moment I kept silent, then I whirled around to face him. "I've heard what your friends say about me."

"What friends?" He tried to look innocent.

"The boys you are with after school." I didn't say shoeshine boys, though that's what I meant. The boys who worked after school shining shoes, I noticed, were not the best students. Often they got in trouble in class, joking with one another and passing notes. Arabella told me those same boys often pestered girls, making rude remarks. And I had observed several of them across the street from the schoolyard smoking cigarettes. Imagine twelve and thirteen-year-old boys smoking cigarettes!

That wasn't what bothered me now, though. A few days before, Arabella and I had gone as usual to Zook's to get a milkshake. Near the entrance, we heard one of the boys mutter something to Esteban, then glance at me. I didn't understand what the boy said, but Arabella did and she told me.

"You – you mean *faceta*," Esteban suddenly stammered. "That just means – *uh* – it means...”

“Snooty or stuck up, that’s what it means,” I exclaimed sharp-
ly. Arabella had told me that’s what *faceta* meant in New Mexico.
In Spain, she said, the word might mean something different.
“Arabella knows all the slang words in Santa Fe and she told me.”
I glared at Esteban. “Anyway, it’s not true. I’m not stuck up.”

His dark skin reddened. “Guys like to say stuff, that’s all.”
He shrugged. “Sorry.” We walked a little further in silence, his
shoulders hunched. Then Esteban burst out, “But you don’t seem
like a regular girl. I mean, remember the first day in the school
cafeteria – you expected someone to carry your tray?”

“I don’t any more,” I responded.

“Maybe not, but Mom says –”

“What does your mother say?” My face suddenly felt hot.

“She’s just surprised she has to pick up your clothes every day
and make your bed.” Esteban shrugged. “Kinda strange for a big
girl like you.”

“But – isn’t that her job?” I spluttered.

“I guess,” he said. “But she’s got plenty to do without doing
that stuff, too. And you could easily do it yourself. Why, you
should see what my kid sister Anita does – cooking, cleaning –
and she’s only ten.”

I frowned. Was it really such a bother for Dolores to pick
up my clothes and make my bed? After all, she was the maid.
Of course, she was not only the maid, she was also the cook, the
cleaning woman, did the laundry and took care of the chickens. I
had to admit – that was quite a lot for one person to do every day.

“And I heard you complain when there’s not enough hot
water for you to take a bath every night.” He looked at me sourly.

"You know how many families in Santa Fe don't have a bathtub? They don't even got hot water in their house."

From Esteban's look, I figured his might be one of those houses without hot running water. No, it hadn't occurred to me to imagine what others didn't have. I tripped suddenly over a little stone. Maybe I truly was *faceta*. Maybe I was spoiled and stuck-up and lazy and didn't even realize it.

"I'll try to do better," I said quite sincerely. "What else did your mother say? Did she mention the horrid crawly insect?"

"You mean the centipede?" he said, pressing his lips together to hold back a smile. "She didn't say much."

The heat in my face traveled all the way down to my toes. I could imagine Dolores and Esteban and the rest of their family laughing at my squeamishness. Perhaps they laughed about lots of things I did and said. For a moment, I could barely speak from embarrassment. But Esteban didn't seem to notice. After a moment, he turned to me eagerly. "You wanna see my ponies?"

"You have ponies?" I was surprised.

"*Uh* well, they're not exactly mine. I'm not sure who they belong to but I ride them."

"Of course I would like to see them," I said. I loved any sort of horse. But also I hoped I could regain some value in his eyes. "I used to go to the stable often," I said, adding, "I'm a very experienced equestrian."

"A very experienced *what*?" He looked puzzled.

"A horseback rider. I'm an excellent horseback rider."

"No kidding?" His serious face brightened. "Then let's go."

He led me across town, through the Plaza from east to west.

This was my first visit to the neighborhood that Arabella called the barrio. She and I had never walked there during our jaunts around town. Right away, I noticed that the houses were smaller and crowded more tightly together. In most yards, chickens ran freely, and in some, I spied a few sheep, goats and even a burro or horse standing in a little pen.

A friendly old man smiled at us from a blue doorway. *"Buenas tardes."* But others on the street looked at me with sharp suspicion. Perhaps my yellow hair and blue eyes seemed out of place. Here, almost everyone had dark hair and eyes and spoke Spanish.

More strongly than any time since my arrival, I felt like a stranger, an outsider, a foreigner. It was a weird feeling. I stuck close by Esteban who seemed to know the neighborhood well. He darted up one narrow twisty street and down another, often speaking or waving to people. And they waved back.

"Do you live near here?" I asked.

He shrugged. "Nah, I live on Cerro Gordo, the other side of town. But I got cousins and friends living around here. It's a great place."

I was pleased, however, when we passed beyond the houses and reached an open field bordered by a rusty wire fence.

"Climb through there," said Esteban pointing to a gap between two wires. He dropped down and crawled through first. After hesitating a moment, I followed, though my hands and skirt got very muddy. I wanted to stop and wipe them off, but Esteban was running across the field. I chased after him through tall scratchy grasses that reached nearly to my waist.

When I reached the other side, Esteban was standing beneath a few old apple trees. Yellow, rotten, gnawed-on apples still stuck to the limbs and littered the ground. Two ponies with shaggy matted coats grazed nearby. Esteban fetched a sort of rope halter with reins that hung from a tree branch. With the clumsy bridle in one hand, he picked up a withered apple in the other. Then he called softly to one of the ponies. "Hey, Diablo, you old *caballo*." As soon as Diablo came close, Esteban slipped on the bridle, grabbed a big tuft of its thick mane and swung himself up.

"You take Daisy over there," he yelled at me. "She's a sweetheart." Then he leaned over Diablo's neck and vigorously kicked the pony's sides, yelling, "Giddyap!"

The pony took off slowly, then galloped down the field with Esteban clinging to its back. He leaned over the mane, holding on tight while kicking and slapping the pony with the rope reins.

Daisy, the other pony, glanced up as the two took off, then returned to munching grass under a tree. Her coat was brown and white, her mane knotted and filled with burrs. She certainly didn't resemble any of the well-groomed ponies or sleek horses I had ridden. Also, I had only ridden with a leather bridle, saddle and riding crop. The groom at the stable, Jonathan, always helped me to mount and dismount.

Even if I could manage to climb on Daisy without a saddle, I feared I might fall off the minute she began to move. What if I broke a bone? That would be so painful! How stupid to have boasted about my equestrian skill! Now Esteban would think I was both a liar and *faceta* if I didn't ride Daisy. He might tell his friends and soon everyone at school would be laughing.

I stepped closer to Daisy and began timidly patting her. She didn't move away or even look up at me. There was something extraordinarily solid and safe about the plump little pony. I leaned against her warm body and put my arms around her furry neck. All my silly worries about what others might think flowed away. Closing my eyes, I felt absolutely secure and content. It was a lovely moment.

"You need a leg up?" Esteban had ridden back and was gazing down at me. His voice was gentle.

"I think not," I said, hugging Daisy again. "We're just getting to know each other today." I glanced up at Esteban and smiled. "I'll ride her next time."

"Hey, that's a good idea, you ride her next time." He looked fondly at Daisy. "She's just an ole' Indian pony, anyway, not like those fancy horses you're used to." He slid off Diablo's back and slapped the pony's side so it ambled away. Then he picked up a shriveled old apple. "Feed this to Daisy and she'll be your friend forever."

I flattened out my palm to offer the apple. Daisy slobbered generously on my hand, then crunched the apple in a few big bites. I wiped the wet stickiness from my palm to my skirt. After all, it was already muddy. Then I stroked Daisy's tangled mane and the pony blew softly into my hair.

"I come here any chance I get," said Esteban. He looked taller than usual and more at ease.

"Do your friends come with you?" I asked.

"Nah, I don't ask those guys to come here," he replied. "You know boys – they sometimes show off and act tough, 'specially in a group. They might try to frighten my ponies. I wouldn't like that."

"You're right," I said. "That would be dreadful."

As we walked home, the light was fading. Esteban talked

about summers when he stayed at an Indian pueblo with his grandparents. "There's ponies there that I can ride any time," he bragged. "And no fences like in town. You can ride all day and not see nothing but maybe a coyote and some snakes."

"An Indian pueblo?" I was unsure what he meant. "Does that mean you're an Indian?"

"Half-Indian. What of it?" he said, a little loudly. "I got uncles and cousins all over the place. In Española and Velarde and the pueblos. Some of us are kinda' mixed up out here."

Esteban sounded bolder than usual, and happier. "Summers are great. We jump in the Rio Grande when we get sweaty hot. Eat squash and tomatoes right out of Grandma's garden. And the dances we do, the dances are –" He suddenly fell silent.

"Dances, tell me about the dances," I said.

Esteban shook his head. "Aw, you come and see for yourself next summer."

"But I won't be here next summer," I replied quickly. "The war will definitely be over by then."

"You think?"

"Yes, of course it will," I declared, though somehow I didn't feel so certain.

Esteban shrugged, then pointed in the distance. "You see those two hills? They're called the Sun and the Moon. Bet you didn't know that." He glanced at me quickly and I shook my head. "Most white people don't. They think the land is just dirt instead of something—something sacred." He looked away shyly.

I looked where he was pointing. To me, the two hills together resembled a woman's bosom, soft and round. Of course, I didn't mention this to Esteban. And I hoped he wasn't thinking the same thing. That would be far too embarrassing!

Esteban accompanied me as far as Clem's house. He stood on the porch a few moments, looking like he wanted to say something more but couldn't find the words. Finally, he said, "Maybe some time we'll go do that again."

"You mean, ride the ponies?"

"Yeah, ride my ponies."

"I'd like that. Really I would."

Esteban grabbed the banister and swung down three steps. Then he took off down the street, fast as when he chased a baseball in the schoolyard. I sighed–boys were so peculiar. If only he was charming more often…

I went over to the mailbox and flipped through the letters inside. Suddenly I saw one addressed in Mother's careless scrawl - and my stomach flip-flopped. Mother didn't usually write. Willy was by far the best correspondent. Why had she written? Was there good news in the letter or…something awful? I tore open the envelope, reading quickly as I walked into the house.

Dear Beatrice:

I hope Miss Pope is taking good care of you. As a nurse, of course, she must be a very busy person. Nurses in England are stretched to the limit. The authorities are desperately looking for more. And you know I would volunteer to help if I had the least aptitude for that sort of thing. But I nearly pass out at the sight of even a few drops of blood, so how could I possibly be of assistance?

I am sure you miss London, but everything here is still awful. The War has not stopped, even a tiny bit.

The bombing of London continues and, frankly, I don't know how the city endures day after day. Yet it does. People help one another, keeping up their spirits in every possible way. I have instructed Cook to make huge pots of soup which we feed to any hungry person, any person who's lost their home. Sometimes there's a line at the back door.

Father is scarcely ever here. He's put up a cot in his office at the War Office and simply lies down for an hour now and again. As for Willy, he had a very close scrape the other day. He had entered a building that had been badly hit. They were trying to pull out some people who were calling for help. Suddenly the ceiling began to fall. A beam hit his head and knocked him out for nearly 10 minutes! Thank God I didn't know of the accident until he arrived home with a bandage on his head. Even then I nearly fainted and required a small glass of brandy to revive. Still, Willy was extremely pleased because they had managed to save several people in the building, and a cat, too.

We trust you are well. Do take good care of yourself. I couldn't bear any other sort of disaster.

Your loving Mum

Folding the letter carefully, my hands trembled and my head felt light. I sank into a nearby chair. It was too horrid to imagine Willy having such a close call and me knowing nothing for days.

I sat for a long time, thinking. Even if I had known, what could I have done? What if I had been right there, could I have actually helped my brother? Or would I have been as useless as Mother, ready to collapse at the mere sight of blood? Fortunately, Willy had been with people who knew what to do. And they had saved his life. I suddenly stood up. I knew what sort of person I wanted to be. I wanted to be the kind who could pitch in and help in any sort of situation.

Yet how did one become that sort of person? You couldn't learn simply by reading a book or talking to somebody. I thought for a moment. Undoubtedly, Clem was that sort of person. And Ana, the girl at the Indian hospital, seemed like that as well. Perhaps I'd meet others. Especially if I was on the look-out for them…

I walked into the kitchen. Dolores was mopping the tile floor. She glanced at me with a nod but kept working. I wondered if she knew about Esteban's ponies and guessed she did not. He seemed like the sort of boy who kept a few secrets. Crossing the damp floor, I noticed that my shoes left muddy tracks on the clean tiles.

Thinking of what Esteban had said, I paused. "Oh, Dolores, I'm dreadfully sorry. Your clean floor is ruined."

She quickly mopped over the tracks. "*No problema, signorita.*"

"Well, I don't want to muddy up the entire house," I declared and sat down on a stool beside the kitchen door. I removed my shoes and found a rag to clean them with. In a moment, my shoes looked quite decent. Dolores glanced over with a tiny sideways smile. I smiled back, feeling quite pleased with myself. I no longer wished her or anyone to think I was *faceta*.

Tiptoeing across the kitchen in my socks, I carried the clean shoes to my room. The big trunk was pushed into the corner of the room. I had removed all my every-day blouses, sweaters, skirts and dresses. But a few clothes remained in the trunk – the sort of fancy dresses which were suitable for attending concerts or parties. I hadn't even wanted to bring them on the trip, but Mother had insisted. "You never know when you may be invited to a special occasion," she said. "And you always want to look your best. Remember Cinderella at the ball."

Frankly, I didn't like to remember Cinderella at the ball. She was not one of my favorite storybook characters. Oh well, I thought, these dresses can remain buried in the bottom of my trunk. I won't need them in Santa Fe. No one here ever dresses up.

Very soon, I discovered, I was completely mistaken!

Chapter Twelve

Uncle Diego is having a party!" Arabella exclaimed, only days later. "Everybody is invited! It's on Wednesday night."

"Everyone? Even us?" I asked. "A party? At night?"

Arabella nodded. "Yes, it's the night before Halloween, but people won't wear masks and costumes. Uncle Diego doesn't care for masks and costumes."

"Still, I can't believe we're invited," I exclaimed. "In England, children are never invited to grown-up parties."

"At Santa Fe parties, anyone can come," Arabella said. "And you never know who might show up – a Hollywood movie star, a mountain man straight from the Rockies, even an opera singer."

I looked at Arabella. I knew she was thinking about her own mother who had been working in New York City for several months. She dialed up her daughter almost every evening while preparing for a performance. Nevertheless, Arabella missed her as much as I missed my own family.

"Do you think Steve will go to the party?" I had thought Esteban might behave differently after showing me his ponies. But he didn't. He still talked almost entirely about baseball or the war. "Indians are warriors," he had explained proudly. "That's why they go fight in every battle."

"Yes, Steve will be there," said Arabella. "Dolores is fixing tamales so he'll bring them to the studio."

"Tamales? What are tamales?" I asked.

"You'll find out," said Arabella with a grin.

"I guess your uncle must be feeling better if he's having a party."

Arabella nodded. "He's finished his portrait of Lola and that makes him feel like she's still around!"

Days before the party, Arabella and I pulled my party frocks out of the trunk, the ones Mother had insisted I bring "just in case." Now they were all mussed and wrinkled but I hated to ask Dolores to iron them.

"Arabella, you may suppose I'm a very dull girl," I said. "But could you show me how to iron?"

Arabella's eyes widened with surprise. "You've never ironed anything?"

I shook my head.

"It's really easy," said Arabella.

We found the ironing board in the pantry and set it up. "That's the hardest part," she explained. Then we plugged the iron in. Arabella seemed to know everything there was to know about ironing. "It's a breeze to iron cotton shirts and skirts," she told me. "But you have to be careful with delicate fabrics like silk or velvet. If the iron is too hot, you'll burn the material. See what I'm doing?" Arabella put a damp towel between the hot iron and the cloth.

"I learned all about ironing from my mother," she exclaimed. "Opera singers wear beautiful dresses, you know."

"I know they do," I said. Once I had gone with my parents to see *The Magic Flute* at Convent Gardens in London. I loved it: the singing, the dancing and all the wonderful costumes.

Arabella showed me photographs of her mother in various roles. "That's her as a beautiful Italian woman in the opera *Tosca*. Here she's a beautiful Spanish woman in *Carmen*."

I gazed at the pictures. "When will she come back here?"

Arabella's face clouded a second and she shrugged. "Her work could take her from New York to Boston or Chicago or St. Louis." She tried to seem lighthearted but her tone was wistful. Like mine when I talked about London.

"When I was a little girl, I stood on a stool and ironed Mom's dresses," said Arabella. "But one time, the ironing board fell over and I got burned badly. I had to go to the hospital. That was the last time Mother let me iron anything for her." Arabella picked up a dress. "Ooh, this red velvet dress is gorgeous! But I can't wear red. Not with my hair."

I held a brown silk dress with a pink lace sash up against myself. "What do you think?" I asked, gazing at myself in the mirror. "Do you fancy it?" I turned around and gazed at Arabella. "Or do you think it makes me look *faceta*?"

"Oh, no, that look is timeless, utterly timeless," drawled Arabella. She sounded just like Lola from Alabama or Scarlett O'Hara from Georgia. "Besides, you can't worry if some silly boy thinks you're *faceta*. You are who you are."

"Perhaps that's true. But –"

"Oh, come on, Beatrice, it's just that you want Steve to like you, don't you?" Arabella's eye twinkled mischievously. "You've got a little crush on him."

"A crush? I certainly do not," I protested. "Of course I want him to like me. As a friend."

Arabella shrugged. "I decided long ago that it's too hard to figure out how to make boys like you. So I quit trying."

"You did? When was that?"

"When I was in fourth grade." Arabella was perfectly serious.

I laughed. Had she really been thinking about boys in fourth grade? Maybe that's what happened when your mother was a romantic opera singer. "But everyone *does* like you. You've got loads of friends," I told her.

"If people like me," she said, "it's because I like them."

It was true. Arabella was friendly to everyone, always smiling and laughing and joking. She wasn't as pretty as some of the other girls, but her smile lit up her face and her dimples were utterly enchanting. Again, I felt fortunate that she was my good friend.

"What's this?" she asked. She'd dug into the bottom of the trunk and retrieved a wadded-up white handkerchief. I looked over with surprise, having forgotten I still had it.

"It's got initials," said Arabella. "R.C.W."

"The last name is Wingate," I said. "I have no idea what the others stand for."

"Well, you can practice your ironing on this," said Arabella. "It's hard to harm a cotton hanky."

The night of the party, Arabella came over two hours early. She helped me dampen my hair and put it in pin-curls so it wouldn't be straight-as-a-pin. She also brought a little pink satin sack filled with powders, lipsticks, eye color and rouges that had belonged to her mother. I stared at the heap in excitement. No proper English girl my age wore even the tiniest bit of make-up. But here in the States, it was apparently considered quite normal. And so why shouldn't I behave as an American?

I applied some red lipstick to my lips as I'd seen Mother do a hundred times. Then I stared at my face. My bright red lips stuck out of my pale face like a clown's. I didn't look beautiful like my mother at all – I looked perfectly ridiculous. In a panic, I grabbed a tissue and rubbed off most of the lipstick. Then I glanced at Arabella. Like an expert, she applied touches of rouge, powder and lipstick to her face.

"Mom taught me how to do this," Arabella explained. "Singers and actresses and fashion models spend hours putting on make-up. It's part of their job." She studied my face a moment and then handed me another tube of lipstick, a soft orangey-pink color. "Try this; it will go better with your blond hair."

Turning back to the mirror, I applied the pinkish-orange to my lips, then gazed at the effect. How pretty I looked. I grabbed the small round pot of rouge.

"Careful, now, a little rouge goes a long way," counseled Arabella. "Just put it here and here." She pointed to spots on my cheeks.

A moment later, I was amazed to see that I looked so very grown-up and attractive. Great-Aunt Augusta would be scandalized! But she would never know.

Just as we were ready to go, Clem walked in. Often she was tired after work, but today she looked especially grey and weary. Still, she looked at the two of us cheerfully. "Hey, don't you gals look pretty." She smiled weakly. "I didn't know you had all those swell dresses, Bea. You been hiding them in that trunk of yours?"

She sneezed and blew her nose. Then she sank into an armchair near the fireplace and flicked on the radio. Usually we listened together to the news about the war in Europe. Tonight I didn't want to. The news was so often terrible these days and I didn't want my mood ruined.

"Aren't you going to the party?" I asked Clem. "We could wait for you."

Arabella elbowed me impatiently.

"No thanks, don't wait for me," said Clem. "You girls go on ahead. I'll come later. Just as soon as I rest up a bit." She sneezed again.

"At least I could get you a cup of tea," I said.

"Aren't you sweet?" Clem said. "But I don't think Arabella is gonna let you stay another minute."

Indeed, Arabella had already half-pulled me outside. "Come on, I can hear the music beginning," she said. "Let's hurry." I waved to Clem and the two of us set off toward her uncle's house. The night was cold and dark. In these final days of October, the nights were much, much colder than the days. When we reached Uncle Diego's house, I suddenly stopped. On top of the long adobe wall leading to Diego's studio were a row of flickering lights that shone magically in the dark.

"What are these?" I exclaimed. Looking more closely, I discovered they were paper bags with burning candles inside.

"We call them farolitos," Arabella explained. "You normally see them at Christmas time. But Uncle Diego wants everyone to know he's having a big party."

Near the entrance to the studio, a throng of people greeted one another loudly. I turned to Arabella. "My goodness, it looks like a costume party. Just look at what those people are wearing."

"Just wait until Halloween, then you'll see costumes," Arabella said. "These are just people in Santa Fe who enjoy dressing up."

Indeed they do, I thought. There was Uncle Diego, normally dressed in his dull dark suit, wearing a little red beret and a short yellow vest stitched all over with bright embroidery. He had on a pair of tight dark green pants, flared at the side like a Spanish matador. Across the room were several women in long green or red velvet skirts, weighed down with heavy silver bracelets, necklaces and belts.

I stared. "Look at all that silver jewelry. I've never seen anything like it."

"That's what Navajo Indian women wear," said Arabella.

"They make the jewelry out of silver and turquoise."

"But those women aren't Indian!" I exclaimed. "They have blond hair and blue eyes like me."

Arabella shrugged. "The clothes are beautiful and very becoming, don't you think? Some people who come here are fascinated by the Indians and want to look like them. Other people want to act like they're Spanish – just wait until Fiesta and you'll see."

I continued to stare. One man was wearing a large furry hat and a leather jacket with long fringe; he had a real dagger strapped to his belt. There were several other men in big cowboy hats and fancy colorful leather boots with shiny spurs. Were they cowboys or just dressing up to look like cowboys?

"I guess people in London don't dress like this at parties," Arabella remarked.

"Oh my goodness, they certainly don't. English men wear tuxedos–identical black jackets, stiff white shirts and bowties."

"I know what tuxedos look like. People sometimes wear them to the opera." Arabella grinned. "They look like a flock of penguins."

"Yes, I suppose they do look a bit like penguins." I said. "And the women at parties all wear lovely long gowns of silk and satin. I've never seen anyone who dresses like an Indian! Why, if they did, they wouldn't be allowed in the door."

Arabella said, "Well, Santa Fe is different. If you had landed in Atlanta or Chicago or Denver, people wouldn't dress like this. People here feel free to do whatever they want and no one much cares."

As she rushed off to greet friends, I considered what she had said. Did people here truly feel free to do whatever they liked?

What did that mean? Was that good or bad? Perhaps some people behaved like that, but certainly not Clem and Dolores and my teacher, Mrs. Montoya.

I began looking around the studio. It had been tidied up for the party. No cans, bottles or paintbrushes were in sight. The guest of honor, of course, was Lola. It was not the real Lola, but her portrait, which reigned over the party. In this large, dramatic painting, Lola was lying on a sofa with a blanket draped across her very shapely body. Her violet eyes seemed to survey the crowd gazing at her, regal as a queen. Beneath the painting, a vase was filled with scarlet roses, the same color as her lips and toenails. Uncle Diego stood nearby like a proud father, talking with guests who admired the painting.

I began studying other paintings by Uncle Diego. Most were landscapes of New Mexico – hills covered with stubby trees, the mountains in the distance. Yet in these pictures the land didn't look bare and desolate, but magical and alive. The colors glowed strongly – purple, blue, gold and red. How could he see something so utterly differently from the way I saw?

Uncle Diego noticed my interest and walked over. "Have you ever painted?" he asked me.

"Never," I replied.

"Would you like to?"

"I'm not sure," I said. "Is it very difficult?"

"Let's see – the hard part, of course, is the seeing, not the painting," he said. "Once you see what you want to paint, then you just have to figure out the right colors and how to make the picture come alive."

"Alive? How do you make your paintings come alive?"

"That's the secret of being an artist." Uncle Diego smiled a crooked little smile. "I hope you try painting some day, Beatrice."

He winked and strolled away toward his other guests. I turned around. The studio buzzed with the noise of people laughing and talking. Live boisterous music filled the air. Five musicians in wide Mexican sombreros and tight pants strummed guitars and blew on trumpets. A little makeshift dance floor was packed with couples dancing.

Suddenly starved, I eyed a long table weighed down with different dishes of food. I spied a platter stacked with odd little packages wrapped in dry leaves. I picked up one and examined it closely

"First you gotta take off the husk," said Esteban, arriving on the other side of the table. He took one of the little bundles, unwrapped the brownish husks and gave it to me with a smile. "I bet you like it."

I took a quick nibble, then another, larger bite. Ooh, ahh! My tongue began to sting! I started fanning my mouth. Tears blurred my sight. Esteban laughed.

"What's so funny?" I exclaimed.

"Quick, a piece of bread." Arabella ran over and handed me a chunk. Then she turned to Esteban. "Didn't you warn her?"

"Hey, I took off the husk," said Esteban, laughing hard.

"Here, let me have that," Arabella said. I handed her the remainder of my tamale and she popped it in her mouth, then greedily licked the red stain on her fingers. "Soon you'll adore tamales like the rest of us." She gestured toward the room. "So what do you think? Isn't this a swell party?"

"Yes, people are having so much fun," I said, looking around the room. Then a thought unsettled me. "But where's Clem? She said she was coming."

"That is strange," said Arabella. "Clem loves parties."

"She does?" I was slightly surprised. Clem was hardworking and serious – so unlike my charming, party-loving Mother.

"Oh, yes, you should see her kick up her heels," said Arabella. "She dances with everyone, even old cowboys."

"Hey, you gals talking about me?" asked an old, dusty cowboy. A second later, I realized he was the same man I had seen at the train station when I arrived. He still had dried mud on his scuffed boots and wore the same shapeless hat. He appeared eager to dance with any female, no matter how young or how old.

"Wanna dance, sweetie?" he asked me, bowing stiffly and putting out his rough paw. I was so surprised, I could barely speak.

"M–me?" I stammered. "You're inviting me to dance?"

Arabella giggled. "Go on, Beatrice, why don't you? Bet you never danced with a cowboy before. That's something to write home about."

She was right, that certainly was something to write home about. Why shouldn't I dance with him? The musicians were playing loudly and the music had a lively, joyful beat. I curtsied and he took my hand in his wrinkled one.

What a great dance partner! He twirled me round and round the room much faster than I had expected. It was such fun! As soon as we'd finished, the cowboy thanked me graciously. Then he immediately turned to Arabella and asked her for the next dance. In a heartbeat, the two whirled away.

Now my foot was tapping to the music. I hated standing there alone. Perhaps I should invite someone to dance? What about Esteban? A delightful shiver ran through me. Oh my goodness, the very idea! Beatrice dancing with a shoeshine boy? Great-Aunt Augusta would be mortified!

I looked around the room – where was he? Drat, I didn't see him anywhere.

Just then I noticed a small Indian girl standing by herself in the corner. Unlike the jolly people at the party, this girl didn't seem to be enjoying herself. In fact she looked rather sad. And her face was familiar. Where had I seen her?

Just then, Esteban squeezed through the crowd of dancers and came over.

"Do you know her?" I gestured toward the girl in the corner.

"Sure do. That's my cousin," he said. "Would you like to meet her?"

"I think I already have," I said, walking up to the girl. "Hello, I'm Beatrice. Do you remember me?"

Ana smiled shyly. "You came to the Indian hospital with Clem."

"I didn't know you were Esteban's cousin," I said.

"I told you I've got hundreds of cousins," Esteban bragged. "All over the place, don't I, Ana?"

Ana nodded. "Yeah, plenty of cousins." She tried to smile, but couldn't quite manage.

"Is anything wrong?" I asked. "You don't seem to be having fun."

Ana gazed at me intently. "Nothing – nothing's wrong."

"Come on, Ana," said Esteban. "Tell the truth. *Que pasa?*"

Ana finally admitted, "I got some bad news today from my

pueblo."

Esteban stopped grinning. "What did ya' hear?"

She turned to him. "Granny is sick and Auntie Delia, too."

"How'd you hear that?" asked Esteban.

"A man from our pueblo came to town yesterday, selling piñons," Ana replied. "He told a relative at the school and that boy told me."

Esteban considered the news a moment, then he scratched his head. "Sorry, Ana, that doesn't sound good."

"Are you absolutely certain?" I asked. "I mean the person could be mistaken. Why don't you ring up your family to find out for sure?"

Esteban shot me an impatient look. "Out on the pueblos, there's no telephone anywhere around. There's no way of learning nothing 'cept when somebody tells somebody else and that person comes to town."

A place without any telephone or telegraph? He was right – I could hardly imagine that. Still, I understood very well how Ana felt. She had family who might be in trouble with no way of knowing for certain. She felt unhappy and helpless. I badly wanted to help, but what could I do?

"Would you like me to tell Clem?" I suggested.

Immediately, Ana's face brightened. "Could you? That's a good idea."

"Of course I will," I said, "right away."

I looked again around the party. Still no sign of Clem. Something must be wrong for her not to come. Maybe there was an accident. Maybe she had to go to the hospital to care for someone.

Still, I would have to leave the party and try to find her. I gazed around the room. The musicians were still blaring on their instruments. The dance floor was jammed with dancers. The old cowboy was twirling around the floor with a woman on his arm as white-haired and stout as Great-Aunt Augusta.

How I hated to leave my first American party. There was more food to taste, more people to meet and more fellows to dance with. I glanced at Esteban…not this time. I had promised Ana. I knew she wanted me to speak to Clem as soon as possible.

"I'll go this instant," I said, running to fetch my coat and gloves from the closet.

A moment later, I glimpsed Arabella. Her face was nearly as orange as her hair and damp with sweat. I figured she must have danced every dance. Now she was eating a large sugar cookie and gulping from a cup of pink punch. She saw that I had put on my coat. "Are you leaving?"

"Yes, I must go," I said, pulling on my gloves.

"Heck, Bea, it's still early. Please, stay a little longer," Arabella pleaded.

"No, I have to go. I need to talk to Clem," I said, glancing a last time around the party. "See you tomorrow. Promise."

"Don't count on it," replied Arabella, turning away briskly. "I may spend tomorrow in bed." And she returned back to the dance floor.

Chapter Thirteen

I ran every step of the way back to Clem's house. I was eager to talk with her. I still couldn't imagine why she hadn't come to the party. Not if she loved dancing, as Arabella claimed. Perhaps she'd just fallen asleep. That often happened to my Father after a long day at the War Office. I would find him in his favorite armchair in the library, peacefully snoring, a book still open in his lap.

I rushed in the door and glanced at Clem's chair by the fire. It was empty, with a mug and a newspaper on the table next to it. Then I saw that the light in her bedroom was still on, so I knocked lightly at the door.

"Come in," said a low, muffled voice. As soon as I saw Clem, I understood why she hadn't come to the party. Her nose was red, her eyes watery. There were several used tissues on the floor around the bed. She had propped herself up on several pillows and was sipping tea from another cup.

She sneezed loudly and blew her reddened nose.

"Yeah," Clem admitted. "I don't feel so good. Nose is stuffed, throat's a little sore. Guess I came down with a bug. Now tell me about the party. I want to hear everything."

Though impatient to give her Ana's news, I first told her about the wonderful party: the line of twinkling farolitos, the people dressed in fantastic outfits, the spirited music. I described eating my first tamale and dancing with the old cowboy.

"Glad you had a swell time, Bea," Clem said. "Sorry I missed the fun. I sure love some peppy music. And you can hardly drag me off the dance floor."

Poor sick Clem, I hated to tell her the bad news. She would feel even worse. And what could she do, anyway, stuck in bed? Yet I had promised Ana and I knew she was counting on me.

"Oh, Clem, I am very sorry to tell you but…" As soon as I finished, she shook her head.

"That pueblo is far away. Most people will be too sick to come into Santa Fe for help."

Clem frowned. "I'll have to go first thing in the morning."

"Go in the morning? But you can't go, you're too sick!" I exclaimed.

She shrugged. "Somebody's got to. Germs don't take holidays."

"But, my goodness, there must be someone else who can help!"

"Not now, I'm afraid. I'm the only one with this job."

I stared at her. The only nurse caring for hundreds, maybe thousands, of people?

"There used to be another public health nurse out here." Clem declared. "Irene Fennipurse was her name. She came from Boston, I believe." Clem sneezed loudly. "I'm not sure how long Miss Fennipurse lasted. But she's not here any more."

"What happened to her?" I asked.

"Being a nurse or a doctor, for that matter, in New Mexico is not for everyone," said Clem. "You've got to make do with what you've got. Pretty much the basics – soap, water, antiseptic, bandages, a stethoscope, a thermometer, a few serums – that's all we've got. And it's not always what you need."

"Where did Miss Fennipurse go?" I asked.

"She went back to Boston or Providence or wherever she came from," said Clem. "She's probably an excellent nurse back there. She just didn't fit in out here."

"So now there's only you?" I said.

"Just me for the time being. Who knows – maybe I'll get some help one of these days," said Clem, putting down her teacup and pulling up the covers. "Now I gotta try to get some sleep. And you, too, Bea. I don't want you catching this darn cold. You need your sleep. You've got school tomorrow."

I was reluctant to leave Clem. I still had many questions I wanted to ask, but she was obviously ready for sleep; her eyes were slowly shutting.

Going to my bedroom, I thought of what Clem had said. Images of Nurse Fennipurse whirled in my head – packing her valise and getting on the train back to Boston. I remembered how I felt when I first arrived. I had wanted to turn directly around and ride the train and the ship all the way home. Barely a month had passed, yet already I felt quite different. What had changed?

That night, I didn't sleep as soundly as usual. I tossed and turned again and again. I felt as if I could see Ana's face and hear her voice calling to me: "Help! Help me, Bea. Granny is sick and Auntie, too. I need your help." In my dream, I wanted to go help her, but when I started to move, my legs didn't work. My feet felt like they were stuck in deep mud. I tried to tell Ana that I was coming, that I wanted to help, but my voice came out high and squeaky, like a child's.

Finally, I scrambled free and began moving toward her. But just before reaching Ana – I saw Esteban standing in my way – a big frown on his face. His voice was loud and jarring: "You can't help, Bea. You're too stuck up, too lazy, too *faceta*!" He kept repeating those words, "You're too *faceta* to help. Too *faceta*."

"I am not. Don't you dare call me *faceta*!" I suddenly awoke, angry and indignant. I wanted to speak to Esteban that very minute. Why did he keep saying I was *faceta*? It wasn't true. Not any more.

I glanced through the window; the light was pale grey. It was still very early in the morning. Yet I could hear Clem moving around her room. She was already getting ready to leave. My bed felt so cozy and warm, I wanted to pull up the covers and stay there. Instead, I threw aside the blankets and ran into Clem's room. She was dressing a little more slowly than usual. She wrapped a long grey silk scarf around her neck.

"Are you really leaving?" I asked. "This very minute?"

She nodded, then sneezed. "Got to go, Bea," she said. "Ana's relatives could have diphtheria."

"Diphtheria?"

"That's a serious disease that used to hit the pueblos every year or two. Now it's much less common. But still very dangerous. Ten, twenty people can die in a very short time."

"But how can you go?" I protested "You're still sick."

"Just a little head cold. It'll clear up in no time."

"How can you be certain?"

"I'm healthy as a horse, always have been," said Clem. She finished dressing and began stuffing a few clothes into her valise. "Never sick for more than a few hours."

Seeing her moving about, I couldn't help thinking how unlike my mother she was. When Mother was even a little sick, she spent a week in bed. She drank herb teas and sipped cups of hot broth that Cook made especially for her. The doctor came nearly every day. Often she insisted I sit on the bed and read aloud poems by Elizabeth Barrett Browning. When Mother was ill, it was a difficult time for everyone in the household.

"Now, Bea, I'll be gone a few days," Clem was saying.

"A few days?" I muttered.

"Don't worry," she said, pulling on her boots. "Dolores will come; she'll look out for you."

"But who will look after you?" The words slipped out of my mouth.

"Oh, don't worry about me. I'll be okay." Clem looked at me fondly. "Like I said last night, there's no one else to do the job. And it's not likely we'll get more help these days, what with the possibility of war. All the help will go in that direction."

"But there must be somebody, somebody who can help you." My mind pitched around, trying to come up with ideas. "What about Ana? It's her pueblo. She could go."

Clem considered the idea. "Ana would probably like to come with me. But she's busy here. The hospital at the Indian School is full of sick kids at this time of year. Plus, I don't think Ana's been inoculated against diphtheria, so she could get sick, herself. That would be terrible."

Inoculated? Suddenly, the most excellent idea crossed my mind. After all, I'd been inoculated in England before I'd come to the States for every possible disease. Father wasn't taking any chances on my staying safe and healthy.

"What about me?" I blurted out. "I could go with you."

"You?" Clem looked surprised.

"I wouldn't get sick," I explained. "I was inoculated with all my shots in England."

Clem paused for a moment. Perhaps she was thinking of the night at the Indian Hospital. I hadn't been any help then, but that wasn't her reason for saying no.

"I appreciate your offer, Bea," said Clem, "but your father had you inoculated because you are very precious to him and your mother. He wants to make sure you're safe. Your parents sent me a long letter telling me just how to care for you."

"I can imagine what that was like," I grumbled. "Especially if Mother wrote it. She doesn't let me go outside if the day is even slightly damp or windy."

"Your parents were very brave to send you across the world to the home of a stranger," Clem said. "They're counting on me to take good care of you. The trip to Ana's pueblo is long and difficult. Who knows what could happen? We could run into all sorts of trouble."

"What kind of trouble?"

"Hail, rain, snow. A bad hailstorm could turn the road to mud. The truck would slide every which way. A snowstorm might blanket us with snow. As for rain, we might be washed down an arroyo and end up in Arizona. There's just no telling what will happen when you take off on a trip in New Mexico."

"Yes, but –"

"Sorry, there's no time for 'buts' today, Bea. I'm in too big a hurry," said Clem. "I gotta go to the Indian Hospital for supplies. I'll come back here, then head out of town for the pueblo. I want to get there before dark." Her voice softened as she started to leave. "See if Dolores is in the kitchen. Ask her to pack up a thermos of coffee with lots of sandwiches for me, okay?"

Clem was already heading for the door. In another minute, she'd be driving to the Indian Hospital. I wanted to say more before she left, but I knew it wouldn't help. So instead, I rushed to the kitchen where Dolores was stuffing kindling in the wood stove. I told her what Clem needed and that she'd return shortly. Dolores quickly got to work on the coffee and food. Seeing Dolores so busy, however, made me feel even worse. She had something useful to do. It was only me who had nothing to do. I hated to stand there feeling helpless.

"Aren't you going to get dressed?" Dolores asked. I was still wearing my nightgown and bed slippers.

"I'll get dressed in a little while," I said morosely. But what was the use now? I might just as well spend the day in bed like Arabella was planning to do.

"Don't you want to eat something, *hita*?" She looked worried. I shook my head. I wasn't the least bit hungry.

Esteban popped through the door, but I ignored him.

"What's wrong?" he asked.

I shrugged. He looked uneasy. "Something bad happen?"

I knew he was thinking that something bad had happened to my family in England. I shook my head. "No, nothing bad has happened. It's just – Clem won't take me with her."

"Clem?" He asked. "Where's she going?"

"To Ana's pueblo, of course. To help with the people who are sick."

"And you want to go?" He looked puzzled.

"Yes, very much," I declared. "I want to help, too."

"You do?" Esteban looked at me carefully in my warm flannel nightgown with a lace collar, then he shook his head. "Nah, it's better if you don't go. You wouldn't like it there."

"Why do you say that, Esteban?" I was so surprised by his words that I forgot to call him Steve.

"The pueblos – they don't have stuff like they do here," he said. "You can't buy a milkshake or even a soda pop. You can't take a bath in a big bathtub with lots of hot water. It ain't like it is here."

"But you love your grandfather's pueblo," I said. "You go there every summer."

"It's different when you grow up there." His lower lip stuck out. "Then you know what it's like. But you, you never been to a place like that. I'm telling you, you won't like it!" He glanced at me once more, then scuttled out the door.

"Esteban," Dolores called after him. But he didn't even bother to stop and get the egg and tortilla she held out for him.

I stood still for a moment. Was Esteban right? Perhaps I

wouldn't like the pueblo. I remembered that night at the Indian Hospital with the boy who was so ill and his somber parents. That night had been a little scary. I also remembered walking through the *barrio* with people staring at me. Did I really want to go to a strange place full of people I didn't know? Sick people, hurt people, maybe even people dying?

Then the dream from last night flooded back into my mind. I recalled Ana's face and how she begged me for help. In the dream, Esteban claimed I was too *faceta* to be of any use. Was he right?

I started to pace back and forth in the hallway. No he was wrong, I wasn't *faceta*. I wanted to go, if only Clem would let me. The clock on the mantel chimed the hour with eight loud dings. Clem had been gone over twenty minutes; she'd be back any second. I ran to my room to get dressed so I'd be ready when she arrived. This time, I would beg her. If she still said no, why, I'd hide in the back of the truck. She wasn't going to leave me behind. Not this time.

Just as I finished dressing, I heard the familiar sound of Maude's engine. Glancing out the window, I saw the truck turn into the driveway. I hadn't yet put on my shoes or brushed my hair as I rushed out the door.

Clem was climbing out of the truck when I arrived. She glanced over. "What the heck are you doing out here in your socking feet? Do want to catch cold, too?"

I shook my head. "Please, Clem…" I started to say.

"You go inside this minute and put your shoes on."

I didn't budge, though I could feel the icy ground through my socks. "No, I won't," I declared. "Not until you tell me I can go."

I saw the hint of a smile in her eyes. "You still want to go with me?"

I nodded forcefully. Even Mary Kingsley couldn't have wanted to head for Africa more than I wanted to make this trip. Clem gazed at me another long moment. "Honestly, kid, this could be the worse decision I ever made. But go fetch your things. We gotta get going! Now! We're late as it is."

I clapped my hands together like a child and started to run to my bedroom. Clem yelled after me, "And don't get that darn trunk of yours, Bea! Grab just a few things – enough to stay warm and dry!"

But when I returned with a handful of things, Clem made me turn back around. "Get a warmer jacket and some pairs of thick socks," she said. "It can get pretty chilly where we're going. And it might rain or snow. It's clear now, but the weather could change any time."

I stuffed a few extra things in my school satchel and brought them out. Clem put the satchel in the back of the truck, next to some other trip supplies: a jug of water, a gallon of petrol, several tools, boxes of blankets and bandages, her nurse's medical bag, a hunk of baling wire and a strong rope.

Clem gazed a moment at the supplies with satisfaction. "That should keep us out of trouble," she said. "At least for a while." Then she put a big box of paper tissues next to her seat. Her nose had grown quite red from all the sneezing.

Just as we were ready to take off, Dolores ran out of the house. She handed me an extra sack of sandwiches and a thermos with hot tea. "*Vaya con Dios*," she said. I had often heard this expression in Santa Fe, "Go with God."

Clem looked at me again. Unlike her usual expression, there

was no hint of a smile. "I hope you know what you're in for, Bea."

I nodded back, brightly as possible. Though in truth, I hadn't the least idea what lay ahead.

Chapter Fourteen

Ten minutes later, we were driving north, out of Santa Fe. I had never been to this part of town. The streets and houses ended abruptly and a bumpy dirt road wound upwards through low reddish hills. Only a month had passed since I first arrived. But it seemed like a much, much longer time. I barely felt like the same girl who had stepped off the train. At that time, I had been an unwilling adventurer, forced here against my will. A very reluctant explorer. Now I looked forward to seeing new things and meeting new people, though I was still a bit unsure of myself and my abilities.

I had insisted, after all, on coming on today's trip. Would Clem be glad she had agreed to take me? I glanced at her, hoping she felt better. She was certainly plucky and unselfish to travel today.

To the east of us, I saw that the mountains were already topped with snow. Seeing these grand mountains gave me the same thrill as the very first time. Clem noticed them, as well.

"My dad used to say mountains make your soul rise up in you," said Clem.

"What a strange thing to say," I said.

"He said all people have souls but we don't always feel them 'cause we're too busy with what's right in front of our noses," she explained. "Then one day you look up and see a beautiful sunset or a rainbow or a waterfall. Suddenly your soul's right there, filling you up."

I turned and gazed again at the mountains. Yes, it was true. I could feel a tingling inside, just as if my soul was bubbling up. I pulled out my little red notebook, writing down Clem's words. They sounded like a poem. I also added a thought of my own:

> Mountains are big but they don't make a person feel small and unimportant. Instead they pass a bit of their grandeur to everything around.

I looked down proudly at my words. How marvelous to think up something original on my own, that no one had told me.

"What's that you got, gal? A notebook?" Clem asked.

I nodded, surprised Clem hadn't before seen it. "Father gave it to me before I came. He wanted to encourage me to be an explorer on my trip here."

"What a smart idea. Has it worked?" She was genuinely interested.

"I wish I took more notes. I often forget," I admitted. "But yes, I do write in it every few days and writing causes me to look at things more carefully. Though I must say I don't always write down just the facts. I write what I imagine, too."

"Whatever you write is good," said Clem. "It's an excellent habit. Keep it up."

And so, despite the bumps in the road, I did keep writing. It seemed like a good way to pass the time.

> 1 November 1940 – On the road
> I can only tell what it looks like here by saying it looks like the moon. Or what I imagine the moon looks like – immense and wide open. The land spreads out in every direction so it's possible to see for miles and miles. Even the ground resembles the moon, rocky and dry, with only pale strokes of green and violet across the dirt. It's so very different from the English countryside with its beautiful green meadows and groves of old trees and grey stone walls that wind over the hills. Though in England you can't see very far because hedges and trees block the view.
> Also here it is so empty – there are hardly any houses, barns, animals or people. Only black ravens soaring high above in the deep blue sky.

I put down my pen and read back what I had written. Indeed, I believed I had described the scenery very well. And that was enough for now, I thought, putting away the notebook.

When I gazed again out the truck window, my thoughts drifted toward London – the busy streets, shops, theaters, cinemas, cozy tea-rooms, crowded trams and speeding taxis. I turned to Clem. "You said you didn't last long in the city. Why was that?"

"Oh my goodness, there are plenty of good things about cities. I love all the different sorts of people, the different languages and food," Clem said. "But in cities, you've also got to put up with the clatter and noise of traffic all the time. And the buildings are so tall you only catch a stripe of sky between 'em. Worst of all, for me was the night, 'cause the city sky is so filled with light, you can't see the stars." She sighed. "That's what I missed most - seeing the stars at night."

"So you came out here to New Mexico?" I asked.

"Not right away. First I was a Red Cross Nurse, then I signed up with the Public Health Service. They sent me to the Rosebud Sioux Reservation in South Dakota. Now that was a tough job. There were Indian children dying of mumps and whooping cough. Diseases that shouldn't kill a kid, not today when we have serums and medicine. But when they haven't had enough to eat or a warm place to stay and maybe we didn't have enough serum to go around." Clem shook her head sadly and her grip tightened on the wheel. Then she reached for a tissue and blew her nose.

"If it was so difficult," I said, "why did you stay?"

"Why?" Clem said, thinking for a moment. "I guess you could call me a sucker. Plus, I grew to like the Sioux a lot. And I learned a lot from 'em. The Indians make many cures themselves with roots and herbs and other stuff. Some doctors ignore that sort of medicine, but it was interesting to me and sometimes useful, too."

"What's a sucker, Clem?"

"That's a good question, Bea." She smiled. "I guess a sucker is someone foolish enough to do things that most clever people won't bother doing."

After that, we both fell silent for a while. Each with her own thoughts. My thoughts returned to England and home. Clem might have still been thinking about the Rosebud Reservation. The sun rose higher, heating up the inside of the truck. Last night, I hadn't slept well and gradually my head started to nod. But suddenly I felt a jolt, as Maude jerked and veered to the side of the road.

"Now what the heck?" exclaimed Clem. She switched off the engine and climbed out. Leaning down, she peered at the front right tire. "Boy, this is a doozie."

She sighed and looked around. "Once I had three flats in one day. Sure hope that doesn't happen today."

I hopped out, too, and glanced around. We were truly in the middle of nowhere. In England, when the tire on our limousine went flat, the chauffeur Henry repaired it. Mother would remain seated in the automobile filing her nails and Father would climb out and smoke a cigarette. Henry always looked very strong and able when he repaired a flat. I gazed up and down the road; no one was coming either way.

"Oh dear, Clem, what shall we do?"

"What do you mean, what shall we do?" said Clem. "We'll fix the dang thing." Whistling a little tune, Clem marched to the rear of the truck and took out some tools. Then she hauled a spare tire from the truck and bounced it a few times on the hard ground.

"Hmmm. This isn't in such good shape, but we'll give it a try."

That's when she looked in my direction. "It's about time you learned how to change a tire. What do you think, Bea?" Before I could even reply, she had handed me a flimsy contraption called a jack. She explained how the jack could raise up the truck so we could safely remove the wheel. By now, the truck was tilting over like a three-legged dog. I asked, "You honestly believe this little jack can lift the entire truck?"

Clem sneezed. "I certainly hope so, Bea. Otherwise, we'll be sitting here for the rest of the day." She blew her nose for emphasis. She knelt down and helped me put the jack under Maude, then showed me how to jerk up and down on the handle. To my huge surprise, the jack lifted up the truck, inch by inch. Clem got out a funny-looking thing called a tire iron. We used the tire iron to unscrew the heavy round lugs that fastened the tire to the wheel. In a short while, we had put on the spare tire and the truck was ready to drive again.

"Well done, kid," she told me. A smile crept across my face.

"How did you get to be so strong, Clem?"

"When I was growing up, housework took real muscle. Ever seen somebody wash sheets by hand? Or carry a heavy basket of wash to the line and hang up wet clothes? Plus, every harvest, we kids hired out as farmhands. Pitching bales of hay under a hot sun is no picnic."

I thought of my life back home, the many idle days I spent reading, doodling or playing with Alfie.

Clem may have guessed my thoughts. "All that time I was working in the house and out in the fields, you know what I wished?"

I shook my head. "I wished I could be lying in a hammock with a good book," said Clem. "I never had enough time to read. I still don't."

By then we were ready to leave, but I had another important question. "Do you suppose we'll be nearing a lavatory soon?"

"A lavatory?" She smiled. "I guess you mean a toilet." She gestured to the sparse bushes and boulders on the side of the road. "Find a spot with a little privacy, that's all there is."

I stared at the bushes without moving. Did she truly expect me to go there?

"Sorry, kid. We won't reach even an outhouse for several hours," Clem added.

An outhouse? That didn't sound very appealing. I peered again at the rocks and bushes. "But what if I encounter a snake or a lizard?"

"A lizard never hurt anybody," Clem smiled mischievously. "But you need to watch out for tarantulas or scorpions. You know what they look like, don't you?"

"Tarantulas are big hairy spiders." I said, shuddering. I recalled a picture in the encyclopedia of this giant ugly creature. "Are there lots of tarantulas around here?"

Clem shook her head. "You might run into one or two during the summer," she said, "but it's too cold right now. I was only teasing you. So do what you need to 'cause we gotta keep moving."

I carefully walked behind a large chamisa bush, pulled down my white silk panties and crouched over. The pee spread across the hard ground like a yellow tide. None splashed on my shoes, thank goodness!

Chapter Fifteen

I hurried back from doing my business behind the chamisa bush. Fortunately, I had not seen a single creature, not even an ant.

Naturally, I walked to the passenger side, ready to climb in. To my surprise, Clem was seated there.

"I was thinking," she said, "if I could get a nap right now, I'd feel a heckuva'lot better. Sleep is the best cure for any ailment, you know." She sneezed loudly and blew her nose. "But it's getting so late in the day, we can't afford to stop here." She looked at me. "Think you could drive for a bit?"

Clem had said lots of surprising things to me during the last month. But hearing her propose that I drive the truck caused my mouth to drop wide open. How could I possibly drive Maude? Why, I was only twelve years old! Clem must be teasing me again. Only it turned out she wasn't.

"I know you're young, Bea, but there are farm kids driving around trucks and tractors who are even younger than you."

"But – but –" I stammered. I hated to say no to anything Clem asked. But truly it was impossible for me to drive! Or so I thought.

Clem looked up and down the dirt road. "The lucky thing is there's no traffic. Maybe a mule or a wagon or two. If we put the truck into second gear, we could bump along slowly for an hour or so. You won't even need to bother with the clutch pedal." She gave me a confident look. "What do you say, Bea? You willing to try?"

Was I willing to try? My goodness, even Father and Mother didn't know how to drive. They relied on Henry for that job. However, Willy had recently learned in order to help with the Home Guard. Of course, he was a young man, five years older than me. Still, I figured, if he was willing to drive in order to help his country in times of peril, then certainly I could do the same.

"All right, I will try. Please just show me what to do." I spoke more confidently than I felt. What if the truck ran into a wagon or an automobile? What if I drove the truck into a ditch, completely wrecking it? What if…what if…the list of potential disasters loomed long and large. Yet I was determined to do my best. Surely, I could manage to drive the truck for a short time without mishap.

Still, as I climbed into the driver's seat, my hands trembled with excitement and nerves. I tightly gripped the steering wheel.

Being tall for my age, I could just peer over the wheel. And by stretching my legs, I could reach the pedals. One foot was on the petrol and one on the brakes, just as Clem instructed me. She said not to bother about the clutch pedal for the time being. But steering was difficult. The wheel was so stiff, even turning it a little took some muscle. Fortunately, there were no big turns ahead.

Once Clem got me started, she wrapped up in a heavy pea-green blanket and settled down on her side as if not worried at all. For a few moments, she watched me guide the truck down the road, then her eyes began to close. Soon I heard her breath come slower and slower. Minutes later, she began to snore as if she were snug in her bed in Santa Fe.

There were no other vehicles on the road. A few black ravens, however, seemed to enjoy hopping clumsily smack in the center of the road. As the truck crept closer and closer, I was certain we'd crush one. But at the last possible moment, the massive birds lifted off the ground and flew away.

Gradually, my fears began to ease. What an ideal place to learn to drive! I was truly getting the feel for it. How amazed my parents would be. Even Willy would be astounded. As for Great-Aunt Augusta, she'd be aghast. Imagine – all of them watching me, Beatrice Sims, driving an old truck down a bumpy dirt road in the wild West!

Time passed quickly. Nothing seemed boring now. I was fascinated by every stone and bush along the way. The land remained open and flat for a while. Then we began winding our way up a mountain slope, up and up. I continued as slowly and carefully as possible. The road had begun to curve, so I couldn't see far ahead. Suddenly, we rounded a bend in the road and a big white goat dashed in front of the truck. Oh my God, how to stop quick! Which pedal to push, which to stop and which to go? I couldn't remember! So I pressed both feet down hard and turned the wheel with all my strength away from the animal. Maude jerked to a stop. The goat was inches from the front grill.

An old woman, dressed all in black, ran forward. She grabbed the goat by a rope collar around its neck and jerked it away. Then she scolded us loudly in Spanish. Though I didn't understand her words, I knew she was furious.

Clem woke with a start and rubbed her eyes. "Where are we?"

We were at the edge of a little village. Along the road were a string of mud-brown houses with steep pitched tin roofs. Next to every house was a pen filled with animals – sheep, goats, pigs, burros and horses. At the end of the village, I spied a charming little church with a white-painted steeple and cross.

"Is this Ana's pueblo?" I asked.

Clem shook her head. "We're in a Hispanic village called Eluardo, about half-way to the pueblo." She stretched her arms. "Golly, that nap did wonders. I feel so much better." We switched places in the truck. Climbing out of the driver's seat, I suddenly felt very tired. Driving had been a thrilling experience, but I was pleased that Clem could take over.

As we continued down the narrow road through Eluard, many people recognized our blue truck and waved. The skinny old lady with the black shawl, however, continued to scowl at us. She dragged the white goat with a rope back to a tiny home on the edge of the village.

"Why is she so angry?" I asked.

"That's Signora Donita," said Clem. "She's the local *curandera*.

150

That means she helps sick people and delivers babies. She thinks a trained nurse like me will take away business."

"Will you?" I asked.

"Not really," said Clem. " As you know, I've got far too many people to care for. So people around here still go to her more than to me. They only call on me when there's a serious problem."

A moment later, Clem pulled off the road at a small house. The building had no more than two or three rooms and a narrow front porch. From the porch rafters hung lots of stuff I'd never before seen.

Seeing me stare, Clem said, "Get out your notebook and I'll tell you what's there.

So I wrote:

> We stopped at a little adobe house in a mountain village called Eluardo. Long chains of bright red peppers hang on all the porch rafters. And rows and rows of dried corn hang there too.

"The people here grow corn and peppers during the summer. Then they dry the peppers and corn to use all winter long," explained Clem. "They've braided the *chiles* into *ristras*. The corn will be soaked and cooked in a stew called *posole*. This family has a good amount of food. They will eat well this winter." She climbed out of the truck and knocked at the door of the little house. A young woman opened the door.

"*Buenos dias*, Maria," said Clem. "*Qué pasa?*" Before speaking, Maria fetched a fat baby and showed it to Clem. She took the baby and held him a moment, looking closely. "*Cómo se llama?*"

"Manuel," the woman announced. The two chatted several minutes in Spanish.

I remained in the truck. A skinny boy came over to the truck and stared at me. His hair was dirty and his eyes were crossed. I looked away, wishing he would leave. Finally, Clem returned to the truck and he backed off slowly. As Maude was pulling away, Maria ran out with a small sack. I rolled down the window and she handed it to me. Inside were big, pale brown cookies, still warm from the oven.

"I delivered that baby on my last trip out here. Maria was having trouble with her labor and she needed me."

"Is it terribly hard to deliver a baby?"

"Depends. Sometimes it's very hard," said Clem. "Still, I love the work – helping a little baby get born is like seeing the bright dawn of a new day." She reached in the sack and handed me a cookie. "I bet you've never eaten a *biscochito*."

We'd eaten the ham sandwiches Dolores had packed long ago. I hadn't realized how starved I was until I took a bite. The cookie was delicious, not too sweet and very crumbly, tasting of cinnamon. I rapidly ate two or three more, then handed a few to Clem. The cookie made me think of English teatime, a special time each day that I truly missed.

"I wish the two of us could stop for a proper tea," I said. "It was always my favorite meal. The only time, really, that my family was all together. Not every day, of course, but often. And there were special treats like fresh-baked crumpets or a treacle pudding."

Clem smiled kindly. "I know how you Brits love your tea. In 1917, when I worked with the nurses from England, they'd light a fire and heat up a kettle, no matter where we were. Even with bullets flying overhead."

I turned and stared at Clem. "You were in England during a war?"

She shook her head. "Just for a short while. I was mostly in France, working alongside some remarkable English nurses. You see, when I was 17, I had a great hankering to get out of Oklahoma and see the world. So I fibbed a little about my age and joined the Red Cross. It was the tail end of the Great War, called the war to end all wars." Dark memories clouded Clem's face. "What a terrible world I saw – full of blood and smoke."

"Yes, I know. That was a horrid war," I said. "My mother's brother died. I never even met him." A photograph of Uncle Charles always sat on Mother's bureau, a handsome young man with dreamy blue eyes.

"A lot of brave American boys never made it back, either," said Clem. "A few of them were just farm boys from Iowa and Kansas and Oklahoma – they knew better how to pull a cow's teat than pull the trigger on a gun. I held their hands and gazed into their eyes right up to the last minute."

Neither of us spoke for a short while. Then I turned to Clem with an urgent request. "You will go again, won't you? Now that Britain needs you?" Tears blurred my vision. "They want every nurse they can get! And you're such a good nurse. You really must go."

Clem reached out and touched my trembling arm. "I'm sorry, Bea, but I don't think I'll be heading overseas again. I've thought a lot about it and I know plenty of American nurses will go. Just not me, not this time. I need to stay here, right where I am." She smiled gently. "But since I like Brits so much, I wanted to help out. That's why I wrote the Overseas Board, volunteering to take in a child."

My eyes widened. "You think that's important? Taking care of me?" I began to shout, "Even now, there are dozens of British soldiers, wounded and dying. Soon there may be American soldiers, too. People who really need your help. How can someone as capable as you are stay here? Just look where we are! Why, there are as many burros here as people!"

Tears ran down my hot cheeks. Clem looked sympathetic, but all she said was, "I do understand, Bea. Honest, I do." We fell silent again and I tried to rein in my feelings. I knew I had no right to yell at Clem. And yet, it was very frustrating...she could do so much and I could do practically nothing.

We had reached the last house in the little village. Clem pulled off the road again. An elderly man was seated on a low bench outside his house. He was dressed in a faded flannel shirt, blue coveralls and a flimsy straw hat. His back rested against the sunny wall of his adobe home. His dark creased face was calm, his eyes distant.

Clem got out and spoke to the old man briefly in Spanish. Then she returned to the truck. "We'll give Señor Baca a ride to the Campo Santo. His wife is buried there. She was sick with tuberculosis for several years and I used to visit. She died a few weeks ago." I scooted over in the seat and Señor Baca climbed in beside me. There was room because the two of us were very skinny.

A little ways outside town I saw a little hillside with a jumble of crosses and gravestones. Stuck here and there in the reddish earth were dried flowers, yellow and purple mostly. The old man climbed out, paused and doffed his hat politely to us. Then he walked over to a mound of fresh dirt topped with a pile of evergreen branches and a small white cross. We watched as he knelt and prayed for a few moments, then Clem put the truck in gear and we rumbled down the narrow road.

In another moment, the village of Eluardo had disappeared completely. It looked as if no one lived anywhere around. The road kept climbing higher and higher and the ruts grew deeper and deeper. Clem looked worried. "Musta' had a big rainstorm, these ruts have gotten much worse since the last time I was here." She steered the truck from one side of the road to the next, trying to find a level place. Dipping and jolting, I recalled the spare we'd put on hours ago – would it hold up?

Suddenly Maude's bottom scraped on the hard mud beneath and the truck stopped, stuck fast. "Gosh dang!" Clem jumped up and down on her seat, while pressing the gas pedal, but the truck didn't budge.

Climbing out, she shook her head. "Drat!" Then she located a screwdriver and turned to me. "You're skinny and tall. And your arms are longer than mine. Climb underneath and poke this around in the dirt until you can un-stick us."

"Me? Crawl underneath the truck and poke around?" I peered down reluctantly.

"It's getting late." Clem gazed with concern at the sun edging toward the horizon. "We wanna reach the pueblo before dark." She took out a rope and tied it to the front fender. "I'll jerk on the truck while you work underneath. Don't worry, the truck can't roll far."

I certainly hoped not. On one side of the road was a steep cliff dropping down to a little stream below. We certainly didn't want Maude to roll in that direction. Grasping the screwdriver, I dropped to my knees and peered under the truck. I would have to lie flat on my stomach and inch forward like a caterpillar.

"I'm going to get absolutely filthy," I groaned.

"Don't worry," Clem replied, "we're not having supper with the Queen."

Taking a deep breath, I lay flat on my stomach and inched forward until half of me was underneath. Barely able to see the stuck place, I jabbed at the hard dirt with the screwdriver. The dirt was hard as a brick.

"Nothing is happening," I shouted up.

Clem shouted back. "Keep at it, Bea. You can do it."

Coughing a little, I stuck the screwdriver into the dirt and jiggled it around. A few tiny pieces broke off, then a larger bit. I stabbed again and again. Finally there ws a pile of dirt next to my nose.

"Good going," yelled Clem. "I can feel the truck shift an inch – we're not so stuck any more."

I crept cautiously back out, coughing a bit. My skirt was so covered with dust you couldn't see the plaid. My red sweater looked brown. Even my blond hair seemed a shade darker. I didn't know it was possible to be so dirty. And what's worse, I knew there would be no chance to bathe. No soap and hot water, not any time soon.

"Okay, Bea, we'll give her a push," said Clem. "That'll get her going."

The two of us stepped behind Maude's rear and applied all the might we could.

In a minute, Maude rolled forward. In fact, the truck rolled clear over to the edge of the road before Clem stopped it. A few feet further and the truck would have gone spinning down to the valley below.

Clem steered Maude into the center of the road. I climbed in beside her and shook my head. A little halo of dust surrounded me. "If anyone sees me, they'll think I'm a chimney sweep," I joked.

Clem didn't seem to hear. Her eyes were set squarely on the road ahead.

Chapter Sixteen

The sun teetered on the edge of the horizon when we finally reached Ana's pueblo. The silence felt like being wrapped in a thick veil. In the nearly purple light, I glimpsed a bent old woman lugging a pail, while another toted a bundle of firewood on her back.

A tall man wrapped in a white blanket, stood on the roof of a round building. He gazed toward the setting sun. Long black hair hung down his back and his face looked strong and serene as if he belonged to the earth and sky.

I shivered. The air was already quite cool. As soon as the sun slipped below the horizon, it would grow colder still. There were no streetlights or telephone lines, only low mud buildings clustered around a large open space. But unlike the Santa Fe

Plaza, there were no benches or grass here; only a few lonely cottonwoods looming high above the bare earth. A forceful wind knocked dried leaves and tumbleweeds against our truck door.

I stared at a beehive-shaped mud mound next to a house. Seeing my curious look, Clem explained, "Those are *hornos*, outdoor ovens for baking bread."

Outdoor ovens? How strange; I tried to imagine Cook baking a plum pudding in an outdoor oven.

Our truck crept through the village. Scrawny dogs barked and snapped at the wheels. Though it was nearly dark, a few small children were still outside playing. They stopped and stared at us. Clem drove toward a small building. It was newer and bigger than the homes and stood a little distance apart. She parked Maude in front.

"What's this?" I asked.

"It's the Indian Day School. I use it when I come to see patients," said Clem. "The young children go here before going to the upper level school in Santa Fe."

"It's a school?"

"Yes, we're just using it as a make-shift clinic. It's the best we can do for now."

I looked around in the dim light. "Where will we spend the night?" My stomach growled.

"Someone will make room for us," said Clem. She jumped out of the truck and grabbed her satchel from the back. I climbed out, too, yawning and stretching. My muscles ached as if we'd been driving for days.

The door of the building opened and a young Indian woman emerged. She rushed over, clearly upset, telling Clem about the sick people inside. Clem listened closely, then turned to me. "Bea, get out the boxes of blankets and bring them inside." She and the woman went into the building.

Glad to have something to do, I started unloading boxes from the trunk. Several children drew close, staring like I was the weirdest thing they'd ever seen. In a minute, they were on all sides. The largest boy spoke in a language I had never heard before. He seemed to be asking questions. I shrugged, having no idea what he was asking.

By now the sunlight had disappeared and the wind was growing stronger. I gazed enviously at the little adobe homes clustered round. Smoke was rising from their round chimneys and light flickered in the small square windows. Why couldn't I be inside one of them and not out here in the dark? If only someone would invite me in…

Pulling a jacket from my bag, I put it on. Then I noticed that none of the children were warmly dressed; one tiny boy had bare feet. I fetched a pair of thick wool socks from my bag and handed them to him. The boy grabbed them and ran off.

I started to carry a box of blankets into the building. But as I neared the door, my feet dragged. What would I find inside? At the Indian Hospital, a single ill boy and his somber parents had frightened me. How terrifying would a roomful of sick people be?

I pulled open the door. Inside, the school appeared to be one large room, dimly lit. The desks had been thrust out of the way. There were no beds, merely blankets and thin mattresses on the floor, each filled with the shape of an ill person. Was Ana's granny here or her Aunt Delia? Around each bed, it seemed as if the entire family had gathered, young and old.

Clem came over. "Why are they here?" I asked, pointing at the families. "Won't they get sick, too?"

"They want to be here, it's part of their tradition. There's no point in asking them to leave – they won't go." She introduced me to her helper, Raya, who was bone-thin, tall and quick-moving. I handed her a crate filled with blankets.

Then I turned to Clem with another big question. What was the terrible smell in the room? I wrinkled my nose – it was worse than spoiled milk or rotten fish.

Clem understood immediately. "That bad smell is diphtheria. The disease itself gives off the odor. I know it's pretty awful, but you'll get used to it."

How could I ever get used to such a hideous smell? I glanced around the shadowy room and shuddered. At that instant, I wished with all my heart that I was back in Santa Fe. Dolores would be putting a hot meal on the table. A letter from England might have arrived in the post. I could sit next to the fire with a cup of tea and listen to the radio. I could take a warm bath, then curl up and read a book or write in my journal. The little house would be cozy and secure. Why had I begged to come on this trip? Why had Clem agreed to bring me? Esteban had been right – I didn't belong here. Not one bit.

Just then, Clem put a hand on my arm. "Grab some blankets and come with me." Her voice was low and steady. She started to walk toward the row of cots and I followed. In the first bed was an old lady so thin her bones stuck out sharply; her skin was grey. Clem sat on the edge of the cot and took the old woman's temperature.

The woman shook all over. Was she freezing cold or feverishly hot? I unfolded a blanket and carefully laid it on top of her. Her eyes opened and her dull gaze shifted from Clem to me. After jotting down her temperature in her notebook, Clem spooned some medicine into the woman's toothless mouth, wiped her damp brow, then stood up and walked to another bed.

I started to leave, too, but couldn't take a step. The old woman had grabbed my skirt and was gripping it tightly. "Please let me go," I whispered loudly. The woman shut her eyes, still holding fast to my skirt. I gulped, frightened and trapped.

"Raya, Raya," I called, as loudly as I dared.

She looked up, saw what was happening and hurried over; she spoke quietly to the old woman, touching her arm. The words calmed the sick woman. One by one, the claw-like fingers opened and I was freed. Not looking back, I quickly moved away.

Walking to one bedside after another, I handed out blankets. People didn't speak but they eagerly grasped the blankets. With each step, though, I felt more tired. I was tired from the long trip, the horrid odor invading my nose, the desperate old woman and the strangeness of everything. I glanced across the room at Clem – she was busy; so was Raya.

All of a sudden, my desire to be helpful and useful crumbled. In another second, I had dropped my two remaining blankets and was heading straight for the door.

Slipping out, cold air washed across my face in a welcome rush. The black moonless night surrounded me, dark as London in the blackout. I knew Maude was close, but I couldn't see a thing. I stared into the dark for several moments. Finally, I made out the shape of the old truck, familiar and comforting. I stumbled over and climbed inside. Finding the green blanket

Clem had used earlier, I wrapped it tightly around me. From the paper sack, I dug out a few pieces of biscochito and greedily stuffed them in my mouth. Then I licked the crumbs on my fingers.

Whether I slept for one hour or three, I had no idea. But I was thoroughly stiff when Clem gently shook my shoulder. "Bea, are you all right?" I blinked, forgetting where I was for a moment. Was I in London? On the ship? In Santa Fe? Then I remembered.

"Yes, I think so," I mumbled.

"We're going to spend the night at Alana's home," she said. "She's Raya's sister. Come with me."

I climbed out of the truck, rubbing my eyes. A thin crescent moon had risen, so there was some light. I could see the little houses; one nestled next to the other. I followed Clem down one path and then another, staying a foot or two behind her. Finally, we stopped at a door.

Before she knocked, I touched her arm. "Honestly, Clem, I am so sorry." My gaze dropped to my feet. "I didn't mean to be such a sissy."

Clem quickly wrapped an arm around my shoulders. "Hey, Bea, I don't need any apologies." Her eyes twinkled. "We all do the best we can at that moment. Now, let's get something to eat, huh? I'm starved as a pole-cat."

I nodded and she gave me another squeeze, then she knocked on the blue door. A stout, smiling woman, Alana, opened the door and we stepped inside. Alana returned to the woodstove and continued stirring something in a heavy iron pot. A baby lay in the crook of her arm; her swollen belly seemed filled with another. Though it was late, two other children played near the fireplace.

Their shiny hair was cut short like smooth black helmets on their little heads. Seeing us, they stopped and stared.

The house was deliciously warm from the woodstove. And the scent wafting up from the black pot seemed almost too good to be true. We had barely settled ourselves on seats when Alana handed us two steaming bowls of beans and chunks of thick white bread. "I have no meat," she apologized. "Ernesto hasn't been able to find much when he goes hunting."

"Beans are fine," said Clem. "Beans are always fine."

I was so famished, I quite forgot any table matters. I gobbled down everything in my bowl as fast as possible, wiping the drips on my sleeve. No food had ever tasted more perfect. Clem ate more slowly. She sat on a low stool watching the children play. Her shoulders sagged a little and the lines in her face showed more clearly. Still, she seemed as calm and relaxed as if she were sitting in her own kitchen.

I envied her ease. How I wished I could feel as comfortable as she in this strange new setting. But how different everything was from the life I knew. For an instant, I thought of the four children I had glimpsed in the London train station. No doubt they were in a nice house with their great-uncle in the English countryside. Nothing startling or unusual would happen to them. Not like it was happening for me.

"Will we drive back to Santa Fe tomorrow?" I asked.

Clem shook her head. "Nope, not tomorrow. Maybe if we're lucky, we can head home the next day," she said. "When people learn I'm here, a lot will show up from all over. Plus there's the sick ones here already that need my help."

For a split-second I felt disappointed, then I pushed aside the feeling. After all, I had chosen to come on this adventure and I needed to be a courageous explorer.

Licking the last traces from my bowl, I peered round the room. There were no closets and only a few pieces of furniture; a rough handmade table, plus several rickety chairs. Clothes, blankets and other belongings were stacked neatly in corners or in baskets that hung from the rafters. A row of brown and black pottery bowls sat along one wall. Inside the bowls, I could glimpse dried beans, apples and nuts.

Once we finished the meal, Alana poured hot water from a pot on the stove into a shallow brown pottery bowl. Clem got out a big bar of green soap. "I bet you'll enjoy this," she said.

"Oh, yes," I said, eagerly scrubbing my face, hands, arms and neck. How nice to be clean again.

With the beans warm in my stomach, I yawned and looked around. Where did everyone sleep? I didn't see any beds. A moment later, my answer arrived as Alana spread several thick blankets on the ground. Yes, on the ground – there was no floor, only dark red earth, packed hard, beneath us. I felt it's smooth surface, warm from the wood heat.

"Know why this earth is red?" asked Clem. I shook my head, not sure that I wanted to know. But Clem couldn't resist telling me. "Ox blood gets mixed with the mud before they lay it down."

"Blood, real blood?" I gulped, staring down at the reddened ground.

Clem nodded mischievously, then rolled up in her blanket and in seconds, I heard her snore. I wrapped the blue and red blanket more tightly around me. The wool was a little scratchy and the floor was very hard. I twitched around for several minutes then I settled into a comfortable position. My last thought was Mary Kingsley bedding down in a pitch-black, damp jungle, amid all sorts of creepy-crawly things, far from anything familiar and English. Yet she was happy as could be…

Minutes later, it seemed, I smelled hot coffee. Opening my eyes, I spied Clem sipping from a mug. Sunlight streamed into the room through two small windows. Clem was chatting to Alana while the baby fed at her bare breast.

"Hey, sleepyhead." Clem remarked as I sat up and rubbed my eyes. "You don't need to get up yet. Alana says you're welcome to stay put long as you want." She drained the last of her cup and put it down firmly. That meant she was ready to get back to work.

Hurriedly climbing out of the blanket, I fumbled with my clothes. "I'll be ready in an instant, " I declared. While I would have enjoyed staying longer in this warm, friendly home, I much preferred sticking with Clem.

"Sure you want to go back there today, Bea?" She eyed me carefully.

"Indeed, I do." I gazed back at her as confidently as possible. But I could understand her concern. What about the awful stench of diphtheria? What about the sick woman who'd grabbed my skirt and the row of silent families? Did I really, truly want to go back?

Somehow, something in my spirit had lifted since last night. And something inside me had settled in as well, a sort of calm determination. "I'm quite ready, Clem," I declared. "Honestly I am."

She didn't hesitate another moment. "Then let's get started." and off we went.

Chapter Seventeen

Ten or more people were waiting in line at the day school. Clem met with each one for as long as needed. She didn't have a proper doctor's office. She was making use of the principal's office where there was barely room for three people. On the table next to her, she kept handy a thermometer, stethoscope, neatly folded pieces of gauze, cotton balls, some salves and ointments, and a big bottle of alcohol.

Raya stood by ready to help. Only a few spoke English. Others pointed and gestured or spoke to Raya who translated for Clem.

When she had a little break between people, Clem spoke to me, "Now's a good time for you to get out your notebook, Bea, and take notes. There's a lot here to learn. Especially if you're interested in nursing."

I agreed – everything was so very interesting! I had left my notebook in the truck the night before, so I ran out and fetched it. I wanted to record as much information as possible.

A boy, nearly as old as me, was first in line. Weak and miserable, he choked on almost every breath. His grandfather explained that the boy had started feeling ill a few days before. He was sweaty with fever, had a sore throat and trouble swallowing. Asking the boy to open his mouth, Clem peered inside. She frowned as she took a cotton swab and quickly dabbed the back of his tongue. The cotton swab was dropped into a glass tube, which she corked tightly and placed in her satchel.

Wishing to see better, I stepped closer, pencil and notebook in hand.

"What I'm looking at, Bea," said Clem, "is the color of the mucous at the back of his throat on his tonsils." She slid a thermometer between the boy's lips. "Of course, we won't be one hundred percent positive until we return to Santa Fe and the lab examines the throat swab, but diphtheria is pretty easy to spot. I can already see a thick, gray-green membrane forming at the back of his throat. That and the smell are clear symptoms," she added.

"Do all diseases smell bad?" I asked.

"Some do, some don't. Diphtheria smells bad like this. Cholera's got its own evil odor. And typhoid's something awful," she explained. "Old-timey doctors used their noses a lot. They didn't have laboratories to test out the germs. They had to figure out what was wrong with a patient from what they saw, smelled and heard of the symptoms."

I quickly wrote down what she said, then nodded toward the

170

boy. "Can you help him?"

"I think so. He's a pretty strong youngster," Clem said. "I'll give him some anti-toxin and that should kick in. As long as my supply of serum lasts, I'll help as many I can."

The line of people didn't get any shorter. As the sun rose higher, people continued to arrive. Some came by wagon, others on mule or horseback; a few patients had walked all on their own. Only one automobile appeared, a much-repaired black Model T that the owner drove very slowly up to the door. Five or six of his relatives poured out. Raya explained that Indians came from other pueblos like Taos and Santa Clara and even Picuris, which was on the other side of the mountains.

Not everyone was sick with diphtheria. An old man pointed to his ankle, hugely swollen and turned purple. He hissed and mimicked a snake biting him to show what had happened. Clem punctured the abscess with a sharp scalpel to let it drain; horrible greenish pus flowed out onto a cloth. Then she applied a lot of antiseptic and bandaged it. Ugly-looking as it was, I tried not to step back. I wanted to see clearly what Clem was doing.

Next she began putting drops into a child's eyes, telling me that trachoma was a problem she often saw at the pueblo. I recorded what she told me.

Trachoma is a nasty disease. When you see girls and boys with pink swollen eyelids, oozing with white gunk, the problem may be trachoma. Most children who live anywhere (even in England) catch it sometimes. But when families live in a place without enough soap and water, then the children can

get sick with trachoma again and again.
The dryness and the wind here are also
very bad for eyes. Sometimes children
go blind!

I put down the notebook and stared at the darling little child. How terrible to imagine her becoming blind. Clem talked to the girl's parents and Raya translated. The mother nodded; she would do her best to take care of her daughter. But with so much wind and so little water, I figured, it would be very difficult.

Next in line was a woman whose skirt was stretched tight across her huge belly. She sat down heavily at the table. Clem felt around her stomach for a moment. "Nothing seems wrong," she said. "The baby's in the right position. You should do fine," Raya told the woman and her husband, a tall handsome man with two long braids down his back. Hearing this news, the two smiled sweetly at one another.

We took a break at mid-day. Alana brought us more beans and fry bread which was a sort of flakey puffed up tortilla and very tasty. While eating, I asked Clem if she would deliver the woman's baby.

"Probably not. She doesn't need me and I might just be in the way." Clem chuckled. "I used to think I knew everything about childbirth. Then I started work on the Sioux reservation. One day I was assisting with a very difficult labor. I was at my wit's end, afraid either the mother or the baby would die."

"Suddenly, in comes this very fat, old Sioux woman with long white hair and a dearskin bag around her neck. She shoved me out of the way and went to work. Less than an hour later, that mother gave birth to twins – both in fine shape," Clem grinned.

"I sure ate humble pie that day."

By the time we'd returned, the line of people outside the day school seemed twice as long as in the morning. There was a girl who'd burned herself falling against a stove and the burns had become infected. Clem carefully applied a salve and gently wrapped the burns in gauze. Then she took a long time instructing the girl's mother what to do and gave her a sack of supplies.

A boy who had broken his wrist came next. The bone had been set in a very simple way and wasn't healing well. Clem told the parents they should take the boy to the Indian Hospital in Santa Fe, where a doctor could reset the break. The parents listened soberly, then left, still talking to one another.

"Will they go to the hospital like you told them?" I asked.

Clem shrugged. "They may. They will if they can. But it's a long trip and they have other children to take care of, plus animals to feed."

"What will happen if they don't go?"

"The boy will do okay, but his hand will always be a little awkward," she said. "I've seen it a lot. Breaks that were fixed without a doctor; sometimes just using a stick or some wire or whatever was handy."

"A stick or some wire?" I was amazed.

"Lots of people in the world don't have doctors," said Clem. "Sometimes there isn't a doctor nearby or they don't have the money for one. People do what they can to survive. That's just how it is."

Clem went to work on the next patient in the line. Raya had returned to the schoolroom. She made space for more sick people, even fixing a few beds on the floor. I wanted to be helpful, so I followed her around like Alfie used to follow me. I helped make beds, swept the floor and tidied up. Anything Raya asked, I attempted to do.

By late afternoon, I felt quite pleased with my efforts. I hadn't been a bother, I hadn't complained and I had made myself useful.

Still, when Clem announced that we might return to Santa Fe the next morning, I was delighted. I longed to return to my cozy room, to the boisterous school, to chatty Arabella and moody Esteban. I missed them all. In addition, I yearned for a hot bath and a cold chocolate milkshake from Zook's.

Then the Indian couple with the sick baby arrived.

Chapter Eighteen

The first thing I noticed was how young the two were. The mother was only a few years older than me, and the boy standing beside her was about the same age as my brother Willy. The girl seemed ill herself. Her smooth dark face showed no expression and her movements were slow and weak. She leaned on the boy to walk.

Still, she clung to her baby, not even wanting to show Clem at first. Raya talked to her gently. Finally the girl handed over the tiny child wrapped in a thin blanket to Clem. The infant smelled awful.

"It must be diphtheria," I murmured, proud of my knowledge.

"Why do you think so?" asked Clem.

"Because of the terrible smell," I said.

"Actually, Bea, the baby does smell bad, but not from diphtheria," said Clem. "She's got dysentery. A very different illness."

Clem asked the couple several more questions as Raya translated. The girl was barely able to speak, so her young husband gave the answers. I listened closely.

We learned the child had been sick for almost a week with continual diarrhea. She had stopped eating or drinking anything a day ago. Now she just lay limp, barely crying or even opening her eyes. The couple had nearly given up hope, sure that their dear little girl was going to die. It was their firstborn, only three months old, and they loved her. The mother had barely eaten or slept herself for almost a week.

I glanced down at the infant. Sick as she was, her face had a very sweet expression. I timidly reached out a finger and touched her soft cheek and stroked her damp black hair.

Clem didn't say much. That was a bad sign. I glanced over at Raya; she was very quiet, too.

"I think we need to tend to the mother as well as the child," said Clem. "Raya, can you explain that to her? We'll do what we can for her baby but she needs help, also." The girl tried to stay, but Raya put an arm around her shoulders. She talked to her softly and led her to a bed in the other room. The father also went to care for her.

"That's good." Clem drew a deep breath. "Now let's see what we can do for the child." She turned back to the baby. "We'll wash her first. That's the least we can do."

"Won't you need hot water?" I said. "I can get some from Alana's house."

"Thanks, Bea, that would be a big help," said Clem. "Fetch a bucketful."

I ran outside, glad to shake off the gloomy room filled with sickness. Outside, the sun seemed especially warm and bright. I looked around – where was Alana's house? The little mud homes looked so similar, same brown color, same blue windowsills and doors. Following Clem last night, it had seemed easy to get there. Now I wasn't sure where to go. I started in one direction, then turned around and went in another. I paused to speak to several people, first an older woman, then a boy of my age. "Excuse me, but I'm looking for the home of a woman named Alana." I spoke loudly and clearly, but no one understood me. They just stared and shook their heads. I had no idea what to do next. I had promised to get water and Clem was waiting for me. Why didn't people here speak English? They lived in the United States, they should speak English – I felt close to tears.

Instead of crying, however, I kept looking. I ran between some homes, then behind a few more. Suddenly, I came upon a little stream; the current was wider and deeper than the Santa Fe River. The bright water shimmered over red and yellow rocks. Close by, I spied a pair of black and white magpies dipping in the water and flicking drops into the air with their long tails. Gazing at them in delight, I almost forgot my errand. Then glancing up, I suddenly saw Alana with her little children tagging behind. She carried two big buckets while her eldest child lugged a heavy pot.

"Alana," I called out and ran over to explain about the baby.

After getting all the water they needed, Alana led me back to her home. She got out a large tin basin and mixed steaming hot water from the kettle on the woodstove with cold water from her bucket.

After thanking her, I murmured, "I'm afraid I might not be able to find my way back." She and the children walked with me most of the way. I carried the basin on my own.

As I returned, Clem led me into a little side room. Though used for storage, most of the shelves were empty. It was a little dusty, but otherwise tidy. There were two old wooden crates to use as a table and seat. Clem put the basin on one of them.

"Have you ever bathed a baby before, Bea?"

I shook my head.

Clem removed the baby's blanket and cloth diaper. Then she began to gently wipe the child's soft skin. I watched closely, eager to begin.

Finally, Clem handed me the cloth. "When we finish cleaning the baby, we'll wrap her up in a nice blanket." Clem paused. "Then she'll look good even if –" She paused for a moment and fell silent.

I gasped. "You don't think she'll die, do you?"

Clem shook her head sadly. "I'm not sure. Right now she's very weak."

"But you can do something, can't you?" I looked earnestly at Clem.

"Sometimes, there's not much we can do." She wrapped a clean blanket around the baby. "And right now, I need to keep working. There are other patients who need me."

"You're...you're just going to let her die?" My heart was

thumping wildly. Somehow the idea of this little baby dying seemed utterly unbearable.

"Bea, we can't always –" Clem repeated.

"But won't you even let me try?" I interrupted and begged, "Please."

It was true that I didn't know how to do much. I had just learned to make beds and sweep the floor and fold bandages. Caring for this baby was an important job. A matter of life and death. Could I really do it? Then I pictured my fun-loving, cricket-playing brother, Willy, pulling people out of burning buildings. If he could save lives, then I could try to do the same!

"Please," I repeated.

Clem took so long to answer me, I was certain she was going to say no. Instead she reached for her nurse's bag and fished out a little dropper and a bottle of clear water. "Sit down here," she instructed. Then she carefully placed the baby in my lap.

"Give her a few drops of distilled water every minute or so. See if she'll take any at all." Clem watched as I carefully squeezed the dropper next to the baby's lips several times. "You understand what to do?" she asked finally. I nodded and she left the room.

Once alone, my confidence slipped. What if I failed? What if I truly couldn't help the child? I imagined the misery on the mother's face. My hand trembled as I again grasped the dropper and filled it with water. I squeezed a few drops onto the baby's lips. The water didn't go in. I used the dropper again and again. But no matter how carefully I squeezed it, most of the water dribbled off, flowing down the baby's chin.

I paused for a moment, thinking, what else could I do? With my finger, I tried to steer a drop or two into the baby's mouth. A tiny amount seemed to go in, though I wasn't positive. Still I kept at it, squeezing the dropper and directing the water to the baby's lips. Thirty, forty minutes passed very slowly. I stared into the infant's face. Could she possibly live? I knew Clem believed there was little hope. How could I keep doing this nearly impossible task? Then the words of Great-Aunt Augusta resounded in my head: "Remember, Beatrice, that you're made of strong stuff. You come from a long line of Duckchesters. Be proud of who you are."

Being proud of who I was did not mean being conceited, stuck-up, *faceta*. I knew Great-Aunt Augusta was saying that she expected a lot from me. She expected me to behave with courage and perseverance. To stick things out — even disagreeable things. That was the fine British tradition to which I belonged.

So I didn't quit, no matter how difficult the task. At first, the baby had seemed light as a feather. But, after a few hours, my arm began to tingle and then to ache. My head started to hurt as well and I grew hungry. The shadows in the room lengthened. Still I kept at my task. Every few minutes, I squeezed another dropper of water on the baby's lips. Perhaps it was my fancy, but it seemed the baby's throat was moving, as if she was swallowing.

Eventually, I heard someone enter the room. Glancing up, I saw Raya. She stood and watched for a moment without speaking then left. A little later, Clem came in; she picked up the baby and examined her closely.

"How is she?" I exclaimed. "Is she any better?"

"To tell the truth, Bea," Clem said, "she's not much better, but she's not any worse."

I sighed. I had hoped for better news.

"Can you keep at it a while longer?" Clem asked.

I nodded. And I did stick to it, much longer than I would have imagined possible. My arm and my legs were cramped, yet I couldn't stretch without putting the baby down. And I didn't want to do that. The light in the room slowly faded. Shadows gathered in the corners. I knew it must be night outside. Still I didn't stop with my task. Finally, Clem and Raya came in together. Clem looked far more tired than yesterday, yet she seemed satisfied with her day's work.

"The baby's mother is sleeping. She probably hasn't slept for days. She ate some, too," said Clem. "I think she'll be all right by morning. Let Raya look after the baby now. You come with me."

I should have felt relieved for the assistance. But it was difficult to give up my little charge. She fit so snugly now in the crook of my arm. At last, I stood and Raya took the baby. Then Clem and I returned to Alana's home.

Though the bowlful of beans tasted marvelous, I was so exhausted, I had to force myself to chew. I could barely wait to wrap myself up in a blanket and stretch out on the hard ground. Once there, I fell instantly and deeply asleep.

Chapter Nineteen

When I woke the next day, it was barely light. Clem and Alana's family were still asleep. Almost immediately, my thoughts flew to the baby. I wondered how she was. I wanted to know. I climbed out from under the blankets. The room was very cold. Only a few grey embers were left in the fireplace. When I poked with a stick, a tiny cloud of smoke emerged, but no flames.

I hurriedly dressed, but still no one was moving. Rather than wait for them, I decided to build a fire in the woodstove. Looking around, I found a few sticks of wood and several pinecones and stuck them on the hearth. Then I discovered a big box of kitchen matches. I struck one and then another, trying to light the wood. It smoked, but there was no flame. I was just about to strike a third match when Alana appeared. She was still wearing the long raggedy shirt she slept in. She took the match from my fingers.

"Please, don't use all the matches," she said, firm but not angry. She showed me how to build a little pyramid with the sticks surrounding a piece of dry bark. Immediately, the fire caught. I warmed my fingers on its little glow. Next time, I thought, I'll be able to make a fire on my own.

Clem was finally sitting up, too, and stretching.

"Hey there," she beamed at me.

"Can't we go to see the baby?" I asked earnestly. Clem shook her head. "Let's eat first."

Alana mixed a bowl of cornmeal batter. As soon as the oil on the iron griddle began to smoke, she spooned out round pale yellow pools. "Now, you try." She handed me the bowl.

My first efforts were a bit of a mess. The children gathered round; they giggled, poked one another and murmured to their mother, who said, "They think that one looks like a turtle and the other one like a frog. But they will all taste good."

I tried to not let on that I had never seen or heard of a griddlecake before that morning. I enjoyed flipping the flat cakes from one side to the other to brown. We made plenty for the two children crowding hungrily at my side. Having only downed a few spoonfuls last night, I was eager to eat as well. And of course Clem had to be filled up with a tall stack doused in honey.

But I could barely wait until everyone had finished. There was only one thing on my mind. "We must go see the baby!" I demanded, restlessly pacing back and forth.

"All right, kid," Clem said, draining her coffee mug.

A minute later, though, as we walked toward the clinic, Clem put her hand on my arm. "It's possible, Bea, the baby didn't survive the night."

My chest tightened as if all the air had been sucked out. As soon as we caught sight of the low white building, I started to run. Inside the little room, Raya had improvised a bed with a crate and a pillow. The baby was lying on her back, very still. My hand trembled as I placed it on the baby's chest, her warm chest – her warm, softly moving chest. She was breathing. She was alive! Alive! The baby was alive!

For a moment, my eyes blurred. Clem gently picked up the tiny child and put her in my arms. "You gotta keep at it. Okay?"

I nodded, my heart now filled with hope. I began giving the infant one dropperful of water after another. She clearly swallowed each. An hour later, sunlight was pouring into the room when the baby first opened her dark brown eyes and gazed up at me.

In fact, she stared at me for a very long time, as if she knew me. By now she was also sucking greedily on the dropper, taking every drop of water I offered.

When Clem had finished looking after her other patients, she came in and examined the baby. She immediately told Raya to fetch the parents. "They aren't expecting such good news. They'll want to come right away."

The young mother seemed far stronger than before. Food and a night's sleep had helped a lot. The baby's father also walked with his head higher. Spying the child in my arms, the girl's step quickened. Yesterday, she'd left feeling so helpless, so hopeless. Now, seeing the baby's eyes wide open, tears flowed down her cheeks.

She gasped and reached for her child.

For a split-second, my fingers tightened their hold on the baby. Then I carefully placed the baby in her mother's arms and the young woman's face lit up with happiness. I felt a pang in my heart and bit my lip hard to stop my tears from welling up. But there were far too many tears to brush aside. As the mother cradled her infant, I ran from the room, blubbering. Out the door and across the pueblo I rushed, my nose running, my shoulders heaving, tears flooding out.

Several people glanced up, but I didn't care. I didn't care how messy I looked or what an idiot I may have seemed. What possible difference did it make? I headed for the little stream at the edge of the village. There I had a big sob by myself for a long while. It felt very good, like a heavy chain had been lifted from my chest. Like a thick flannel blanket smothering my heart had been pulled away.

An hour later, Clem found me sitting next to the stream, watching the water leap over the gleaming, yellow and red stones. I had already splashed a lot of cold water on my red cheeks but I still felt bleary-eyed. Clem put an arm around me and squeezed hard. "We've done about as much as we can on this trip," she announced. "It's time to go back to Santa Fe."

What welcome news that was! I still felt filthy from my excursion beneath the truck. I ached from the tiring work of the last few days. How lovely it would be to step into a steaming hot bath. How pleasant to climb into a bed with real sheets.

As we walked back toward the pueblo, however, I paused to listen. There was a sound I'd never heard before, as strong and deep and steady as the heartbeat of the earth.

"What's that noise, Clem?"

"Hmmm," she listened too. "It sounds like an Indian dance. Maybe we should stay for a while."

Moments later, standing on the edge of the large bare central space, we watched. First a band of twenty or thirty old men appeared from behind a round building. They walked very slowly, beating big drums and slowly chanting in low even tones.

Then two buffalo, or what looked like two buffalo, appeared. They were really men wearing big shaggy buffalo heads, with black-painted chests and leather britches. Each was bent forward with his hands resting on short sticks so it seemed as if he had four legs, not two. As the buffalo-men walked, they switched their shoulders and hips from side to side, just like wild beasts. Behind the buffalo came four deer dancers. Large antlers adorned their heads, deerskin covered their shoulders and shaggy little tails hung from the backs of their britches.

Ending the procession were a line of stately young women in black tunics and white embroidered shirts. Each wore a painted wooden headdress adorned with evergreen boughs. Belts of little shells jingled as they moved. Their feet, clad in white leather boots, tread softly to the rhythm of the drums. One of the young women looked very much like Ana. Yet I knew Ana must still be far away in Santa Fe. Perhaps, she's a sister or cousin, I thought.

Though the sun rose high in the sky, the dancers didn't seem to tire. They danced steadily, timelessly, as if no one were watching. As if they were dancing for the sky and the earth alone. Finally, as mysteriously as they arrived, the drummers turned and began walking away with the dancers following. They all disappeared into a round building at the edge of the pueblo. The dance was over.

In a few minutes, everything returned to normal, with people carrying wood and water, children playing, and dogs barking.

"We were lucky to see that, weren't we?" said Clem as we headed toward the truck. "It doesn't happen every day."

"Why do you think they were dancing?" I asked.

Clem shrugged. "Maybe 'cause the illness seems to be over, at least for now. So they were thanking their spirit gods."

"But it was you and your serum, not the spirit gods, that stopped the sickness from spreading," I exclaimed.

She laughed. "Oh, you could say it was both the gods and me that did the work."

I recalled how Esteban had described the Sun and Moon hills in Santa Fe. "They're not just dirt – they're sacred." I paused for a moment, thinking. Maybe everything was some of both – ordinary stuff *and* spirit.

A few minutes later we began repacking Maude with what was left of the supplies. People from the pueblo crowded around; a few told Clem of ailments that hadn't been treated. She nodded sympathetically. "I'll get back soon as I can."

Most had come to bring us things: baskets of squash and dried chile, fresh eggs and dry corn, a rabbit skin, a beaded necklace. One old lady even tried to make us take a live lamb. When Clem said we had no place to keep the lamb, the old woman became so angry she waved her walking stick in the air. Clem finally calmed her down by taking a basket of wool.

After saying our good-byes again and again, we climbed into the truck. Maude bumped slowly over the rutted track out of the pueblo. I was very pleased about returning to Santa Fe. And yet twisting around for a last look at the big cottonwood trees and dusty square, I had an odd wistful feeling.

I turned back around in the seat. "Do you remember, Clem, how upset I got when you told me you weren't returning to England as a nurse?"

"I remember," said Clem

"I was very upset."

"You sure were."

"I simply couldn't understand," I repeated, "why you wouldn't want to go over there and help when there's a big war going on."

Clem nodded. "Uh huh."

"Yet now that I've seen you here," I said, gesturing back to the pueblo. "it seems as if you've found another war to fight, a different sort of war." I paused, thinking hard. "People need help here, too, sick people, old people, children, babies. Someone must care for them," I declared. "If everyone went off to the war in Europe, who would do that?"

For once, Clem didn't come up with a quick reply. Instead she reached over and squeezed my shoulder, smiling at me like an old friend.

The trip back to Santa Fe didn't seem half as long as the trip to the pueblo. For one thing, we didn't have a flat tire and we didn't get stuck on mud ruts in the road.

I napped quite a bit as Maude rolled along. Clem's cold had nearly disappeared except for an occasional sneeze. After a few hours, we pulled off the road near a large clump of chamisa bushes. Each found a sheltered spot to do her business.

As we walked back to the truck, Clem paused and gave me a keen look. "You know, Bea, I wasn't at all sure about bringing you on this trip."

"I know you weren't," I said. "What changed your mind?"

"Driving back from the Indian Hospital, I started thinking," said Clem, "it's about time Beatrice Sims shows us whether she's got any starch in her or not. Then when I saw you run out and stand there in the cold, I figured, we had better give you a chance."

I considered this for a moment. "So what do you think now? Do I have any starch?"

Clem didn't speak for several seconds. She stroked her chin and appeared to be pondering the question. I knew she was taking so long just to tease me. Finally she grinned. "You sure do, Bea. You showed us that you've got quite a bit of starch for a gal your age."

Climbing back into the truck, I felt a warm feeling bubbling up from inside. And as I settled into the passenger seat, my back felt much straighter and my shoulders felt a bit higher.

"Ramrod straight" is the expression Great-Aunt Augusta might have used to describe my posture. In fact, I believed she would have been very pleased to hear about my conduct. Even an ancestor as distinguished as the Earl of Duckchester might have been impressed.

Chapter Twenty

Dolores' cooking had never smelled so good. It was long after dark by the time we pulled up to the door. Dolores had stayed late to make sure we had a hot dinner. I could hardly wait to sit down and eat, but Clem insisted I take a long bath first and scrub thoroughly.

As I settled back into the hot water, I realized how incredibly special a bath could be. I had never imagined anything so wonderful. What if I had to haul buckets of water and heat them up on a wood stove as Alana and her family did every day? Not just for baths but for afternoon tea or simply to wash the dishes. As I climbed out of the bath and wrapped myself in a clean thick towel, I thought – I am a very fortunate girl. A very, very fortunate girl.

At dinner, I piled so much food on my plate, even Clem

noticed. "Take it easy, kid," she cautioned with a grin. Of course, her plate was brimming, as well.

The following morning, when Esteban came in the kitchen door, he seemed particularly glad to see me, but also rather shy. I had decided, however, that I would not say one word about the trip until he asked. The two of us walked almost the entire distance to school before he finally spoke up.

"So what did you think?" he muttered in a voice so low I could barely hear.

"What did I think about what?" I replied innocently.

"Well, now you've seen an Indian pueblo, betcha you ain't ever going back, are you?" Esteban's eyes studied the ground at his feet.

I paused. What should I say to him? Of course I could say that the pueblo was truly a wretched place. There was the nasty smell of diphtheria and the old lady who'd grabbed hold of me. There were the skinny dogs chasing one another and the boy with almost bare feet in the cold night air.

Yet I remembered so many other things, as well. The dignity of the tall man on the rooftop gazing at the sunset, kind, dedicated Raya, the warmth of Alana's home and her children's laughter, the sparkling stream with magpies, and the Indian dancers. Plus all the people crowding around us when it was time to leave, filling our hands with food and gifts. Having carefully considered everything, I decided Ana's pueblo was an excellent place – one I cared for nearly as much as my own precious London – even though the two were completely, utterly different.

"Oh, Esteban." His Spanish name just slipped out. "It was a

terrific trip. Fabulous! I would go back to Ana's pueblo, or to any Indian pueblo, any time that I could. Any time I was invited."

Esteban's somber face lit up. "Gosh, you thought it was okay? You – you liked it there?" he exclaimed.

Suddenly he was filled with ideas. "Well, then you gotta visit my grandfather's pueblo. Come next summer when I'm staying out there! We'll do some neat stuff. Swim in the Rio Grande, ride ponies. Hey, I'll teach you how to fish. Bet you never even caught a fish." He reached over and squeezed my hand a second. Then turning bright red, he bolted down the sidewalk for school. I didn't even get a chance to say I wouldn't be here next summer.

Minutes later, I met up with Arabella. Unlike Esteban, she wasn't the least bit shy about asking questions. "I want you to tell me everything," she demanded. "What did you eat? Where did you sleep? Is it true there's a terrible epidemic?"

I patiently answered each of her questions. Also, knowing how much she enjoyed exciting adventures, I described our harrowing experience on the steep mountain road. Arabella's eyes grew large as I told of bravely crawling under the truck to free Maude from the dirt rut.

"And then, the truck almost hurtled over the side of a cliff!" I exclaimed. "With both of us in it!" A bit of an exaggeration, but worth it because Arabella was speechless with admiration.

Telling her about the first evening at the pueblo, however, I felt a bit embarrassed. "It was so very dark and cold. I wasn't helpful at all – I ran and hid."

"What do you mean, you weren't helpful? There's not one girl in ten who would even consider a trip like that," Arabella said. "I doubt I would. There are too many things I need to be comfortable."

After school, she talked me into going to visit Uncle Diego and telling him of the trip. Surprise of surprises, whom should we see when we entered the studio? None other than Lola! She explained that she'd returned from Hollywood on the train. "The weather jes' didn't suit me out there like I thought it would," she drawled. "And there were no gentlemen as fine as your uncle." She looked very fondly at Uncle Diego.

In her lovely pink and blue kimono, her long black hair flowing down her back, Lola lolled on the sofa again. She appeared quite content to be back in Santa Fe. Meanwhile, Uncle Diego moved about the room, quick as a boy, gathering paints and preparing for another grand portrait of her.

Arabella insisted I tell my adventures all over again to them. Lola and Uncle Diego acted suitably impressed, but they were clearly more interested in one another than anything else at the moment.

I did know who would be pleased to hear about absolutely everything. A few days later, when Clem was going to the Indian Hospital, I asked to go with her. I saw Ana almost immediately. She was folding laundry into a tall stack. As soon as we arrived, her eyes lit up. She wanted to hear every detail of the trip. She was especially interested in the fate of the sick baby. "You nursed her all by yourself? For almost two days?"

I nodded proudly, then asked, "How are your aunt and grandmother?"

Ana smiled. "They are much better. Most people at my pueblo are well now."

We could have talked longer, but Clem had finished checking on the patients and we had to return home.

"Could you come back again?" Ana said. "I'd like to show you the school so you can meet some other girls. There are students here from almost every pueblo."

"Yes, of course I will come back," I replied quickly. How amazing to have such a special new friend.

We had returned just in time for the United States Presidential Election. And I wanted to put in my journal exactly what happened:

> I have some very good news to report. On 5 November, the American people re-elected Franklin Delano Roosevelt as president of the United States. He will be the first president in American history who serves for a third term. Of course, that creep, Donald Riggsbee, was not the least bit excited. He said: "Roosevelt only won by 20,000 votes in New Mexico. Lots of people voted for Willkie."
>
> So I said to him, "You don't think 20,000 is a lot of people? Why, the entire city of Santa Fe is only 20,000 people at present." That shut up Donald.

Clem and I both celebrated Roosevelt's re-election. She was particularly happy that so many programs for poor people would continue. And I knew that the president and the U.S. Congress would be helping England as much as possible.

But about a week later, I received a letter from my Father in England with rather painful news.

7 November 1940
My Dearest Beatrice,

We have both good news to tell you and news which may make you rather unhappy. The good news is that the awful bombing in London has stopped for the present. The Brits showed all the world how strongly united we are against our enemy. With the re-election of President Roosevelt, we hope to get help soon from our friends across the ocean.

Now for the rather bad news. The War in Europe and here is still going on strongly. We'd all hoped for it to be ended quickly, but that's not the case. At the present time, there are no passenger ships crossing the Atlantic in either direction. It's too dangerous. There are far too many German torpedo submarines cruising about, ready to attack.

So although we are longing to see you again and I'm sure that you're longing to see us as well, that won't happen as soon as we'd all hoped. Please try to keep up your spirits and make the best of everything. All of us, including Alfie, who I promise is fine and Great-Aunt Augusta, too, send you our very best.

With all my love,
Father

P.S. By now, I am hoping that you have filled the pages of the notebook I gave you and you need another one. Don't delay. Please purchase one and I will send you the additional money.

I have to admit when I had finished reading the letter, my feelings were very muddled. On the one hand, of course, I was terrifically disappointed and sad that I was not going home straight away. Christmas was fast approaching. How could I bear to spend this lovely holiday away from my family?

No one had imagined that the war would drag on so long. The beastly Nazis were being horrible to the English and to the French, Poles, Dutch, Danes and many others. Why, the war was taking a terrible toll all over Europe. It was a ghastly mess.

At the same time, there was another feeling inside me. I must be quite honest in stating that I was not entirely unhappy. As much as I missed dear old London and my family, I had become quite fond of this odd little town called Santa Fe.

In the last few months, I had grown to appreciate many small things like tortillas and milkshakes, even tamales. Much more importantly, I had begun to care for Arabella, Esteban, Uncle Diego, Ana and, of course, Clem. They had all become very dear to me. Plus, I was very busy. In addition to schoolwork, I made my bed every morning, helped with the dishes, fed the hens (sometimes even cleaned out the henhouse – a disgusting job), shoveled snow off the porch, polished my shoes (with Esteban's help) and other jobs as needed. Nothing very grand, to be sure, but enough to make me feel quite different from the "little princess" who had arrived here with a big trunk, not so long ago.

Clem put it very nicely. "I believe you've begun to feel your oats, Bea."

So, I wrote a letter home:

13 November 1940

Dear Father, Mother, and Willy,

Your news does make me unhappy. As you see from the blobs of ink, quite a few tears fell on this sheet of paper as I started to write. But you should also know that Santa Fe is not so ghastly as I first thought. It's true the houses are mud and flat on top and many streets aren't paved. Practically no one makes a decent cup of tea and I am forgetting proper table manners. At the same time, most folks (as Clem likes to say) are very nice. Also I am constantly seeing, learning and doing new things. Enough to fill the pages of my notebook!

Also, I've discovered there are things that are nearly impossible to describe in words. Like the Indian dance I saw at Ana's pueblo with the drums and the deer and buffalo dancers. How fortunate I was to see that. As soon as the war is over, I hope you can come and see for yourselves. Perhaps by next summer or surely by next fall? Then you can meet Clem and Arabella and Esteban and Ana. What a real hoot we'd all have!!

Your loving daughter,

Beatrice

Clem and I spent a good deal of time together these days, though naturally she still had to work hard with no extra help. And she certainly wasn't going to get any with everything extra going toward the war in Europe. The United States was not yet in the battle. But all American men between the ages of 18 and 45 had to register for the draft, just in case they needed to serve. The news in the newspaper and on the radio was filled with terrible stories, such as the bombing of the cathedral in Coventry on 14 November. The entire little town was destroyed. Father had been right, no place in England was safe.

Meanwhile, our lives here remained carefree. One Saturday in late November, Clem and I went downtown to the elegant Lensic Theater to see *The Wizard of Oz*. We had heard the new movie was super. Clem was especially interested because the film featured a farm girl named Dorothy. Farm girls are much the same, she claimed.

Before showing the film, a newsreel appeared on the big screen. It featured England's brave leader Sir Winston Churchill as he spoke to the United States Congress. His stirring words made my heart beat fast:

"Here we are together facing a group of mighty foes who seek our ruin; we are defending all that to free men is dear. Twice in a single generation the catastrophe of world war has fallen upon us; twice in our lifetime has the long arm of fate reached across the ocean to bring the United States into the forefront of the battle. Sure I am that this day, that the task which has been set us is not above our strength; that its pangs and toils are not beyond our endurance...."

By the end, Clem and I were both wiping tears from our eyes. And to my great surprise and delight, many in the audience clapped for Mr. Churchill. Then President Franklin D. Roosevelt appeared on the screen. He explained that he was sending big battleships and supplies to help out America's best ally, England. That's when I stood right up in the middle of the theater and gave a big hurrah for FDR!

Then we watched *The Wizard of Oz* which was enchanting. And in color! The very first color picture I had ever seen. Clem told me she had seen a big tornado in Oklahoma. Her family hid in the cellar, just like Dorothy's family.

Afterwards, Clem and I went to Zook's and ordered giant ice cream sundaes with hot fudge and whipped cream. Outside, the temperature was well below freezing and snowflakes were flying in the air. "Most folks order hot chocolate when there's a blizzard outside," complained the skinny girl who carried our sundaes to the table.

A few minutes later we walked down the street with our heads bent low toward the cold. Clem paused in front of a store. "You know, Bea, since you're going to be here for a stretch, we gotta find you something comfortable to wear."

A short time later, I gazed at myself in the store's mirror. I saw a thin, rather pale, very blond girl wearing sturdy blue denim jeans, a plaid flannel shirt and a belt with a wide silver buckle. I stared back into the girl's grey eyes. Who would have guessed Beatrice Agatha Sims could look like this? Why, this Beatrice resembled an explorer like Mary Kingsley. Or a cowgirl like Annie Oakley!

And that wasn't the end of it. Clem helped me pick out a pair of boots. Not just any boots, either. I selected shiny brown cowboy boots with red and yellow trim and pointy toes. What my French tutor, Madame Dépeche, might have called *la piece de la résistance*.

I couldn't resist wearing the whole outfit home, even though the narrow toes on the boots pinched a bit. Clem promised they'd soon feel as snug as a pair of old slippers.

Walking out of the store, we spied the same crusty old cowboy whom I'd seen at the train station and with whom I had danced at Uncle Diego's party. He doffed his hat cordially as we passed. My cheeks suddenly felt warm indeed. Why, anyone seeing how the two of us were dressed might think we were related!

Every day after school, I put on the boots so I could break them in. Of course that meant I needed a good place to wear them. One day, on my own, I decided to find the field where Esteban's ponies grazed. It took more looking than I had imagined. I walked up and down the winding narrow streets in the barrio neighborhood. I still looked different from the folks who lived there. But now I could say *hola* – Spanish for hello – to anyone I passed. And everyone returned the greeting with a smile.

Fortunately, I was wearing a thick jacket because the weather was piercingly cold; a thin layer of snow covered the ground. At last, I found the hole in the fence and climbed through. It was far easier than the first time because I wasn't worried about getting mud on my trousers. Clem had told me, the denim jeans were meant for tough times and rough conditions.

Soon I stood next to Esteban's shaggy ponies, Diablo and Daisy. They glanced at me and returned to munching the long grasses, fringed with icy droplets. I poked around on the frozen ground until I found a withered apple. Then I grabbed the rope bridle from the tree.

"C'mon, c'mon, little horsie," I crooned, coming up to Daisy.

Then, while the horse munched the apple, I put on the bridle, grabbed a piece of her mane and pulled myself up. Daisy's back felt warm and wide beneath my legs. She quickly put her head down to eat more but I jerked hard on the reins and kicked. Daisy lifted her head and took a few steps forward.

I kicked her again, leaning forward and whispering in her furry ears, "Go, Daisy, go. I want to ride like the wind!"

Daisy reluctantly broke into a trot and then, with a little more urging, she cantered, or 'loped,' as they say out West. I had to grip tightly with my knees to keep from sliding off. Though it was not as easy as sitting in an English saddle, I stayed securely on Daisy's back. A few moments later, I pulled her around. The pony slowed down and ambled back to the patch of ground under the fruit trees. I let her drop her head down to graze, but remained astride, taking a deep gulp of the cold air.

It was a simply gorgeous moment, being astride a warm pony in such a splendid place!

Yes, it is splendid, I thought, gazing around. It's beautiful here. To the east, the mountains were tinged with a warm lavender glow – a reflection of the setting sun. To the west, the sun hovered at the edge of the horizon. The tremendous sky was layered with colors – first crimson, then purple, then streaks of pink and finally a slim gleam of gold between earth and sky.

Gazing at the sunset caused something inside me to swell with wonder.

"Why, I believe those are the very colors in Uncle Diego's paintings!" I exclaimed. Daisy's ears pricked up at the sound of my voice. "To think I never noticed before! I never believed that anything quite so marvelous could be real."

A moment later, I slid off Daisy's back, both feet landing solidly on the ground. I patted the pony's shaggy coat once more before heading home.

Author's Note:

Both girls and boys came to Santa Fe, New Mexico, from England during World War II (1940-1945). Four girls, for example, were hosted by the John Gaw Meem family. They were among thousands of children who were sent to Canada, the United States and Australia to escape the war.

Beatrice Sims is a fictional character as are her friends Arabella, Esteban and Ana. The pueblo and small Hispanic town are also fictional.

Beatrice's host Clementine Pope is based on a public health nurse named Elinor Gregg, who wrote a book called *The Indians and the Nurse,* about her experiences among the Rosebud Sioux. Miss Gregg retired to Santa Fe and hosted two boys during the war. However, Clementine Pope is a fictional character.

Certain liberties have been taken with historical facts. For example, Winston Churchill did not address the U.S. Congress until a later time.

For their help, I would sincerely like to thank

Nancy Meem Wirth for sharing her story and for editorial assistance: Consuelo Gonzales, Barbara Mayfield, Diane Bird, Lasita Shalev and Gail Snyder.

I also want to express my admiration for all the bold women who served as public health nurses dedicated to improving health care on the pueblos and Indian reservations during the last century.

About the Author

Rosemary Zibart works as a journalist, playwright and children's book writer. She created the first in a series of travel books for youth called *Kidding Around San Francisco*. Her newspaper and magazine articles tackled issues such as how art can transform the lives of at-risk teens and the Heart Gallery that promotes the adoption of children and teens. She also writes award-winning plays for adults and children like *My Dear Doctor* about the first woman physician Elizabeth Blackwell. Rosemary lives in Santa Fe. In 2004, she received an "Angel in Adoption" award from the National Coalition on Adoption Institute. Learn more at www.rosemaryzibart.com.

True Brit - Beatrice, 1940 is the first in a series about the experiences of children during World War II.

CPSIA information can be obtained at www.ICGtesting.com
Printed in the USA
LVOW081659031012

301362LV00013B/51/P